TESSA HASTJARJANTO

Tales of Lunis Aquaria

First published by Narratess 2019

Copyright © 2019 by Tessa Hastjarjanto

First edition

ISBN: 9789083006529

Editing by Anna Reel
Cover art by Emma Hastjarjanto
Editing by Raven van Dijk

Contents

Introduction

The sun is setting. The bright blue of the sky changes in a warm orange before it turns navy blue. Twilight slowly turns into night and the voices of the birds fade away.

To the West, a moon shows itself, chasing away the clouds that block its light. The tree casts a shadow in the moonlight. On the other side of the tree another shadow appears. To the East, a second moon appears from behind the mountains.

The reflection of light reveals the surface of the moons moves. It's hypnotizing, how the moons seem to glitter.

A meow comes from the bushes and a moment later a large feline with fur as dark as night sky jumps out. The silver spots on his fur have the same patterns as the stars above.

The air behind the feline moves and changes color. The ethereal image of a woman appears without becoming solid. Her lips move as if she wants to say something.

"Welcome to Lunis Aquaria"

The coming of beasts

In the earliest of times, there was a celestial being who was referred to as the Lady. If humans knew of her existence, they would surely worship her as a goddess. She rarely showed herself to any living being, but she cared for the land. Her energy flowed through the ley lines crossing the lands, helping the world grow and evolve. She had the power to stop a drought or increase the fertility of fish. She never created miracles but only nudged nature into the right direction.

This went on for years. Vegetation flourished, and evolution set in for the existing animals. Civilization spread, although slowly. She didn't mind; she enjoyed watching humanity grow to a thriving civilization. It would take several millennia and not without setbacks. That was a part of life, she learned. The best civilizations survived war, starvation, and natural disasters. She didn't like it, but it was necessary. It was by her choice she didn't always interfere with calamities. Necessity and danger were a large source of inspiration for human invention. Conflict and setbacks would allow the world to become stronger, and that's what she wanted — a strong world, able to take care of itself.

Decades passed, and she kept the balance. Before she first reworked the ley lines, power gathered where the lines crossed.

Nature bloomed, and animals gathered naturally around these spots. Fruits were juicier, bigger, and had a brighter color. Evolution slowed down in these areas because the conditions were too perfect, and nothing had to adjust.

Humans didn't always notice the power, but they felt drawn to them unconsciously. Villages grew around the power sinks, and people felt better when they were close to these places. The power seeping through had a positive effect on people; in some rare cases they even developed gifts beyond their human abilities.

The power sinks also affected the growth and mutations of the flora and fauna in the immediate area. Flowers changed color. Fruits gained healing abilities and a rich flavor. The animals looked slightly different and had better senses.

The Lady left a few of these power sinks while she restructured others. Every world needed extraordinary places. She was also curious about what would happen in these places.

Throughout the centuries, her guidance lessened. The world had adapted to a point of independence. Now, the Lady filled her days with meditating in the sunshine. The grove where she lived was small, but it was the largest power sink. Meditation allowed her to tap into the ley lines and feel how the world was developing.

During one of her meditation sessions, a feline jumped from a shrubbery into the clearing. He saw the Lady lying on the ground. He stalked towards her with caution, circling her to see what he was dealing with. When he determined it was safe, he approached her face. He sniffed and pushed his head against her hair. Soft purring came from his small body. The feline curled up between her arms and went to sleep.

The Lady woke up with the sun burning down on her and found her new friend between her arms. She felt an instant connection with the little creature. She never saw anything like him. He reminded her of the night sky with his dark blue fur with silvery markings. His tail was long and fluffier towards the end. He used it as a pillow. He had a pointy snout and ears, looking slender and soft. She patted his small head. The feline woke up and looked at her. In his silver eyes, she saw a shimmer that looked like a nebula.

"Hi Nebula. Do you want to stay with me?" She scratched him under his chin.

The feline meowed and purred, enjoying her attention. A smile appeared on the Lady's face. She had found a friend when she thought she never would. Most creatures paid no attention to her, and she didn't know whether it was because they couldn't sense her, or that they didn't care for her. She hadn't received the gift of mind reading like others of her kind.

Nebula was different. He stayed close to her and demanded attention at the most inconvenient times. He would push his head against her hand or lick her toes. If a squirrel was nearby, he would chase it until it grew tired. He never killed in front of her. The Lady blew leaves in the air to give him something to catch. It was his favorite game in the fall.

The feline disappeared most nights. He was a night crawler, active only when the moon and stars reflected in his fur. The Lady still spent most days in meditation, and he slept at her feet during the day. Nebula made her life a little more exciting, and she adored him.

They often looked at the moons together. One was much larger than the other and the patterns changes as the flow of the water did. The coloring in Nebula's eyes also changed to reflect the patterns of the moons. Even during an eclipse when a moon glows red or blue, his eyes changed. The Lady loved that about him. He was so in tune with what happened in the sky; she wondered if he was a celestial being as well.

It was rare to see the moons close to each other as they were usually on opposite sides of the sky. Those nights they crossed each other, Nebula stayed as close as possible to the Lady, as if he was trying to protect her. The Lady hadn't figured out why since she didn't notice any significant events during those days. His behavior taught her to be more alert on these days.

During a day before the moons crossed, the Lady noticed she had otherworldly visitors. Five observers were left on her world. She found out their purpose was to find more places which could be inhabited by their own people. The observers were created to report back to their home planet. Through hardship, they had proved immortal. They had self-healing powers and were resistant to diseases. They couldn't die nor be destroyed.

The Lady didn't mind the observers and was entertained by them. The observers were fluid and lacked the senses they needed to experience the world as it was. They moved awkwardly and slowly, taking in as much as possible but not efficiently.

The Lady was curious to know how they saw the world and if they spotted anything she couldn't see. A few years later she asked them to share their observations with her in exchange for additional power and access to the ley lines. This power would allow them to do their job more precisely and extensively. They accepted her offer as they had nothing to lose.

The five observers came to her in a glade deep in the midland forests. They formed a circle around the Lady in the clearing. Nebula peered at the five creatures from a distance. The observers stood there silently when the Lady began her chant. Their fluid appearances slowly became more solid. Ancient words of power filled the silence of the forest. Power built up around her, and she redirected it to the creatures. They were given the shape of an animal the Lady remembered from a previous incarnation. In these shapes they were to roam the planet and see how life was developing.

One was given wings so it could observe the skies and the world from above. One was given fins so he could observe everything in the waters. One was given speed so he could travel swiftly. One was given the ability to dig so he could observe what was going on below the surface. The last one was given patience so she could observe one thing and follow its complete life cycle.

When the creatures' appearances finalized, Nebula emerged from his hiding spot and greeted each of them personally. All five nodded back in recognition. They knew Nebula was special to the Lady. He gave off a different vibe than other life forms they had encountered. But not even the Lady knew what he was exactly. Nebula hadn't aged over the years, and the observers told her they hadn't seen anything like Nebula, as if he was the only one of his kind.

The five observers—a phoenix, a dolphin, a fox, a wolf, and a bear—thanked the Lady for her generosity and went on their way. The Lady didn't know what to expect from their collaboration, but she looked forward to seeing them again.

The sacred maiden

There once was a girl who lived in a cottage at the very edge of a small village with her parents. Her father was a woodcutter, and he needed enough space to store the logs, so living near the forest made his job easier. Her father sold the logs he brought back from the woods to the neighbors. One of them was a skilled carpenter, and they would often work together to make furniture. Her mother did woodcarving when she wasn't doing work around the house. She carved small decorative statues of animals out of the small branches that couldn't be used for construction work. The girl often helped her and received compliments on her carvings from the villagers. They said her carvings seemed alive even when they were still a bit rough. Her mother knew that she would one day be an artist.

Once a week the girl and her mother would go the market to sell the carvings and purchase their necessities. The girl would sit with the figurines displayed on a crate and talked to the villagers who came by. Sometimes other children would come by to look at the beautiful carvings. Her father took her out on other days, educating her about life in the forest. He pointed out small creatures, trees, edible berries, and the dangers in the woods. He taught her how to track down animals but never how to hunt because she was still too young. The little girl and her father often played hide and seek in the woods between her chores. Both her parents loved her very much. Although they wanted a sibling for her, it never happened. Her parents lavished her with attention and affection, giving her everything she needed and wanted. The girl, even though she'd only seen ten summers, was grateful for all her parents did for her.

One night, a group of bandits came to the cottage. They wanted money. When they saw the small amount her parents gave them, they weren't satisfied. They were convinced there were other treasures hidden inside the cottage, like jewels or family heirlooms. The bandits killed the girl's father when he said there wasn't anything else — that they weren't materialistic — and beat up her mother when she tried to protect the little girl. Having gone unnoticed so far, she tried to escape. Just as she snuck out of the window, the guy who stood watch outside the cottage saw her, yelled to his comrades, and chased after her. But she knew the forest better than most people and was confident she could hide from her pursuer.

She knew of a natural well, deep within the forest where she could hide for the night, and she knew how to get there fast. It had always been her favorite hiding place when playing with her father, and he had never found her there. A grown man would have difficulty taking the same path as it involved crouching through a small opening between some rocks.

The darkness was another advantage. Her pursuer didn't know the forest, so he fell and stumbled often. The girl heard him calling after her, cursing the trees when he tripped over their roots, and the stones when his feet bumped into them. When she reached the opening between the rocks, the man nearly caught her, cursing as he saw her light nightgown disappear into the darkness.

The girl knew it was only a short run from the rocks towards the big, hollow tree that stood beside the well. The old oak was strategically placed between thorny rose bushes and poison ivy, and she had made a small opening in the shrubbery to reach the perfect hiding place years ago, returning there often to make sure it was still big enough as she grew taller. Wearing a nightgown left her legs exposed, poison ivy would scratch her as she crawled inside, but she spotted and picked a few purple flowers to treat the itching before she crawled in.

As she moved through the bushes, she heard the bandit screaming for her. With a surge of panic, she rushed through. The end of her gown got caught on the thorns, tearing away, but she didn't notice until the man had entered the clearing. The piece of cloth hung at the corner of the bush and didn't reveal that she had passed through the undergrowth instead of moving away from the clearing. A fox ran out of the bushes close to the girl. The sound distracted the man; he followed the sounds of the animal and left the clearing again. The girl was relieved when she didn't hear his footsteps anymore, but too scared to come out and so, eventually, she fell asleep from exhaustion.

The next morning she woke up and the aches in her body, her dirty gown, and the hard surface beneath her reminded her the robbery and chase had been real. She remembered what those men had done to her father, and she hoped her mother was still alive. Tears welled up, and some found their way to her cheeks. She knew she shouldn't cry because she wasn't safe yet. What if the bandits were still looking for her? They would come back here because it was the point her trail had ended, and she couldn't protect herself if they found her. She had to reach her neighbor's house and then find her way to her uncle

8

and aunt's place. That's where her mother would've gone to, if she was still alive. Going back was not an option. She didn't want to see her dead father, and the bandits might still be in the area.

The girl listened to see if anyone was around; she heard birds singing, so she thought it was safe. She came out of her hiding spot, carefully, and looked around. Seeing no one, she took the chance to eat some berries from the bush closest to the well, washed her face, and drank to take the edge off her thirst. But when she looked up from the water, she saw the reflection of a man standing behind her. He grinned, grabbed her by her neck, and forced her into the brook until her lungs filled up with water.

The man tied a heavy rock to the little girl's body and threw her into the well where no one could find her. He left the clearing, searching for his way back to the cottage. His friends would still be there with the food and ale they'd found. As he went, he realized the way back was far from easy because there was nothing he recognized from the nightly chase.

After nearly an hour of fruitless walking, he heard branches snap behind him. Slowly, he turned to see a giant stag with massive antlers; its head towered above the bandit, looking at him. The creature pounded its hooves and moved towards him, speeding up with every step. The man was petrified. He tried to move his legs, but his body didn't respond to any of his impulses. The stag leaned forward, and its great, sharp antlers pierced the man's body on impact.

An eerie voice, almost indiscernible from the wind, told the man his life would serve as payment for his crimes committed against the girl. His friends would be served the same fate after they left the cottage. The girl was sacred to this forest because of who she was and how she came to be. She was part of the life of the forest, had come from the forest. Her parents had accepted this gift before she was born, and her fate had always remained tied to that of the forest. Her death would kill the forest, but the bandits' sacrifice would bring life back to it. Their ignorance in not seeing who she'd been had cost him his life and the lives of his friends. Life did not leave his body until after he had heard the stag's message.

The stag led her uncle to the well and helped him find her body. The stag told him what had happened and that the girl should not be forgotten. Her spirit stayed, because it was her duty. She told her uncle the whole story. The man cried as he lifted the girl's body from the water. He brought her back to the village and shared the story about her misfortune and the bandits with everyone. In time, the villagers built a shrine and named her the guardian of the forest. They knew she was close whenever they saw the stag. From then on, the villagers often received help in the forest when needed, and all that was evil or bore ill will was kept away, all to keep the village safe.

Moon flower

There once was a boy who fell in love with the prettiest girl in the village. She was also the kindest, always ready to help someone in need. He wasn't the only boy who fancied her, and every time he tried to woo her she turned away, as she did with all the others. It was difficult for her to choose the right man from all of her suitors, and her father thought no one was good enough. The boys only showed her their best sides and their best qualities, but she knew that every man had a side that wasn't as graceful. Her own father was a man with an ugly side. Her mother regretted the choice she'd made and told her daughter to watch out for it. She wanted her daughter to get to know her future husband before they wedded. That's why she never responded to all the praise and gifts. She wished the boys would be themselves and also let her see their weaknesses.

The boy one day asked her what she wanted if not gifts or compliments. She said she only wanted a man who would do the impossible for her, not once, but forever, hoping that that would scare him off. The girl didn't know what it was she wanted, besides honesty. But if a boy was honest and showed his real self, what kind of personality did she hope for? What imperfections would she accept? She knew what she didn't want: someone like her father. He was a drunk who disrespected his wife. The girl was everything to the boy, and he did everything he could to keep her close.

Apart from honesty, she didn't say exactly what it was she wanted. The boy had heard of a legend of the most beautiful flower growing in the mountains. It only bloomed during a full moon, but when picked with a blooming flower, the flower would never wilt. That was the power of the moon. He decided that this should be her gift, as a token of his love, forever blooming for her. It would be enough to gain her attention.

He told his father of his plan, and his father told him not to go. The mountains were dangerous, and the moonflower story was nothing more than a fancy tale a bard told him on a drunken evening. Flowers like that didn't exist, and it was useless to risk your life for something like that.

His father told him that animals weren't the only danger in the mountains. At night, even the wolves wouldn't come out of their shelter. The boy asked his father why. He had never heard of wolves fearing anything, even bears didn't scare them. His father told him of people who lived inside the mountain. These people didn't look like the villagers; they were short and had a sturdy appearance. Their heads were harder than rock, so they wouldn't die if a rock fell down on their heads. Their faces looked weird because the eyes were the size of a small child's hand because of the lack of light inside the mountain, and the noses were bigger than a human's. But worst of all, they ate everything. Even their own kind. Meat was scarce inside the mountains, so they hunted for meat during the night to avoid bright sunlight. They couldn't see the difference between a human and an animal outside, so they hunted anything that breathed and smelled edible.

The boy shrugged off the warning as a legend, just like his father had dismissed the story of the moonflower. He had heard this story before, from the village elder. The elder had also whispered that these people were just a myth to scare little children from going into the woods at night. His father asked why he believed in one story and disregarded the other as a myth; both were equally unlikely to be true. The boy said having tried to find the flower would be enough to convince the girl he would do the impossible for her. Flower or no flower.

The boy continued to plan his trip into the mountains. He went to the blacksmith to buy the tools to climb a mountain and told him his story. The old man also warned him. The boy said his father already told him about the man-eating people, but he still wanted to go. The blacksmith told him more. When the mountain people didn't eat meat, they ate rocks. That's how they created their homes. They ate the rock, their teeth harder than any metal the blacksmith had ever used. He showed the boy a tooth from one of these people. The tooth was over a hundred years old, having been handed down from father to son. The blacksmith used it to puncture holes in metal plates. It was the only thing that could penetrate them. The blacksmith's grandfather had found the tooth in the mountains.

Although it was daytime, the blacksmith's grandfather heard strange creatures moving about. It was the only thing he heard, all the other animals had gone silent and hid themselves. Then he saw the mountain people from far away. They were eating one of their own. Its clothes ripped, blood flowing everywhere. The only reason he got away with his life was because the wind came from the opposite direction, so they never smelled him. If they had, he wouldn't have survived. Days later he returned to that spot and found the tooth.

It was the only time someone had ever seen the mountain people during the day. The blacksmith guessed their eyes had grown shut, or they were completely blind to not be bothered by the sun. They must have had a good reason to go outside in daylight, and the man thought it had something to do with their dead kinsman.

The boy waved the story off as something that happened long ago and was still determined to go. This girl was worth the risk. She was beautiful and smart, her smile could brighten any dark day. She had her own opinions, but these were never thoughtless. The boy went to the grocer to buy the rest of his supplies. He needed food, matches, and better clothes. The grocer asked him where his journey was headed. The boy told him, and again he was warned. The man still told him another story of the mountain people.

The grocer had been expecting a merchant with luxury goods, but the merchant had never arrived. He asked around and even sent a messenger to the other village to ask if the merchant had left. They had told him the merchant had left weeks ago and that he had wanted to go through the mountains because it would save time. When the grocer heard that, he feared the worst. He knew the merchant was alone and only had his wagon and horse with him. If he really did go through the mountains, there wasn't a chance he made it through if he had encountered the mountain people. Every week he would go look for the merchant, but found nothing. Almost a year later he heard from a hunter he had found some jewels in a cave. That's when the grocer knew that the merchant and his horse had been eaten. Apart from the jewels that were found, all the merchandise was gone.

The boy still wanted to go, but he needed a weapon. Maybe the mountain people were a myth, but the danger of wolves and bears was definitely real. If he encountered one, he could defend himself with it. He wasn't certain a weapon would aid him against the mountain people. They couldn't see and their skin was harder than rock, so he decided that he would target their noses. They hunt with their noses, so any foul smell should keep them away. He bought rotten fish to cover himself in at night. He would breathe through his mouth, and hopefully he would wake up again.

A few days before the next full moon, he left. His father said his goodbye in tears, fearing his son would not return. The girl had heard of the boy's plan and waved him off from a distance. This gave him the courage he needed to continue his quest. The first two days went well, but these were just the outskirts of the mountains. He needed to reach the summit. It would take at least two more days for the most dangerous part of his journey. He feared rockslides the most. No tool could save him from a broken neck. Every night he would cover himself in rotten fish.

One night the boy heard something. The leaves rustled, and a branch broke. Something large and heavy came his way, but it was only one creature. He knew it wasn't the mountain people because they moved in groups. A soft growling came from the creature. The boy didn't move and kept his eyes shut. He heard it move closer as he sniffed the fish. Its nose moved around the fish, probably trying to find a fish that wasn't rotten. The boy felt the creature's warm breath through the fabric of his pants. The warmth was welcome on this cold night, but he feared that the creature would prefer his legs over the fish.

The nose found the boy's leg. His pants soaked up the

moisture from its nose. It might have been only a second that its nose touched him, but the boy wished his death would be swift. He heard a grunt that reminded him of an animal. A wolf? A bear? Its presence felt large enough to be a predator. He closed his eyes and wished the creature gone. The sound disappeared, as did the nose. The boy relaxed, still waiting a moment before taking a breath again.

He hadn't seen nor heard the mountain people, he thought. Maybe they had only ever been stories after all. The tooth could've been from a bear or wolf, and the merchant could've been kidnapped by robbers, or wanted to start a new life.

After two days of climbing the mountain, he reached the summit. The sun was setting, its light left long shadows through the few trees bordering the clearing. The rest of the summit was covered in flower beds, grass, and a small creek was streaming down the mountain. Its water was clear, cold, and refreshing when the boy drank from it. It tasted sweeter than what he was used to. The grass was also greener than in the pastures around the village. It was the evening of the full moon, so the flower had to be blooming there somewhere.

After the sun went down, the moon appeared, but it wasn't full yet. The boy waited patiently, fighting against his sleep. A few hours passed, and a flower bloomed. Not just one, as he expected. Near his feet a flower opened and reflected the moonlight. The mute petals turned into a bright pale blue in the dark. Their reflective light made him squint. He closed his eyes for a second, and when he opened them again, the entire summit of the mountain was glowing. It was a magical thing to behold, and he knew that this moment would be more beautiful than any day with the girl of his dreams, for she had no magic like this. It looked like the lake during a summer's day, reflecting the sunshine on the clear blue water. He dug one up with some earth still attached to the roots and stashed it away in a leather pouch carefully. He covered himself in fish and went to sleep.

Little did he know, that was the last time he would see the moons or the sun, or the flowers bloom for a very long time. The rocks around the summit moved and the patter of feet approached the boy. Dark shadows hung above him. The boy woke up, but the strength of the creatures was enough to hold him down without a problem. They carried him away into the dark of the mountain.

A week had gone by, and the father of the boy worried. He didn't expect him to be back yet, but he had a bad feeling. The man had nightmares about the mountain people. Although he didn't know what they looked like, they were always present; they were always after him. Another week passed, and still there was no sign of his son. No one in the village had seen him. Even the hunters had seen no traces of him coming down the mountain. His father knew he would never see his son again.

The next full moon, the girl was awoken by a sound outside her window. When she opened it, there was a pot with the most beautiful flower. There was a note attached: 'This flower represents my love, blooming forever for you'. The girl knew who it was from, but the boy was never seen or heard of again. She knew he was alive and was sad to lose the only man willing to go such lengths. The girl now knew what she wished she had: a man willing to sacrifice everything for her. And she lost him. The girl married another man but never loved him truly.

She later gave birth to her daughter and told her the story of a foolish boy with a foolish love.

Thomas and the wolf

The screams from the people inside were endless. Behind the trees red clouds lined the night sky. The smell of burning wood and charred meat filled the air. The barn was alight. Flames had already reached the top of the roof and licked the canopies of the trees.

The whole village had gathered for an emergency meeting, and it was the only building that could fit everyone. Something was wrong with the crops, and fruit bushes in the area had died. Food was scarce, which was why the village had gathered. A decision had to be made, but it was already too late. The worst-case scenario happened, no one had come out of the barn.

An enormous wolf stood watch at the edge of the forest. He arrived after the fire started. His silver fur reflected the orange and red colors of the flames which made it look like a sunset. He decided he needed to stay until the unrest was over. There were people still screaming for themselves and for their loved ones.

There was one voice, Wolf noticed, that was different. It was a man, his voice less desperate, but more protective. He kept shouting for Thomas. "You were right. Stay safe. Run. Never return here. I love you." Wolf's ear twitched. This Thomas wasn't in the barn; he was still alive. Probably the only one who would live after this incident.

"That's my name—Thomas. And that was my father." And just as the young boy said it, the roof of the building collapsed, and the screams ended. He was standing next to Wolf and sighed.

Wolf turned his head. He didn't hear anyone approaching him. That had never happened before. Thomas just stood there, watching the fire.

"I warned them, told them not to go. But they never listen to me. Why would they? They know everything, and I'm only eight summers old. Nine now, if a new day has started." The boy was skinny with hair almost white; his face was pale with red cheeks. A strong jawline, high cheekbones but shallow cheeks pointed towards a lack of food. His light gray eyes showed no emotion, just like his voice. Wolf had never seen a human with such coloring before.

The boy looked at Wolf. "You also knew this would happen, didn't you? Why else would you be here? I've never seen you around before." The boy stared into Wolf's eyes. It didn't seem to matter Wolf was more than twice his size. There was no fear in the boy's eyes. Wolf lowered his head to level with the boy. "No, I didn't know like you did. I felt a disturbance, and I needed to find out what it was. I can see the aftermath, but what has caused this?" The growling of Wolf sounded clearly in Thomas's mind.

"I thought you would know because of what you are. I guess I was wrong. I can tell you what happened, but I can't say why right now. The decisions made by the elders always seemed without reason. Do you know what kind of place this is?" Thomas spoke as if he was years older than he was. It confused Wolf.

Wolf nodded once. He could feel the power. Anyone could, but not everyone would know what it was that they felt. His task as an observer didn't allow him to interfere, but Thomas had recognized him. He didn't know what to do with the boy, but there was someone who did.

"The ley lines cross in this area, and the barn itself was built exactly over the powersink. The building blocked off the only way for the powersink to release its excessive power. It formed a bubble filled with energy under the barn, like a blood blister. Once it popped, all the energy bursted out at once. A blister just releases blood and fluid, while this caused an explosion." The boy kept looking at the barn. Small red sparks flew up into the night sky, which was filled with black clouds from the ashes.

"What caused the energy to release so suddenly? Surely they didn't know." Wolf stared at the boy, trying to figure him out.

"No. I told them, but none of them believed me. I don't know what happened, but I can only imagine. Our mayor has a walking stick, and he always bashes it on the floor to silence everyone. Maybe he broke the floor doing so.The explosion is harder to explain. I think it has to do with the speed and amount of energy released on the wooden structure. I don't understand it, but I do know the power."

Wolf nodded and turned his head towards the barn. "You know you cannot stay here. It isn't safe. The negative energy will corrupt you." Wolf's ears turned towards the boy.

The boy sighed and nodded. "I knew you would say that and I'm in no position to question you. I already felt the effects the last few weeks. You know what I am and what I can do. Bring me to the others so you can decide my fate."

Wolf turned around and walked deeper into the woods, away

from the massacre and smoldering wood. Thomas followed him closely. "Are you sure you want to go now? You loved your parents. Don't you want to say goodbye?" said Wolf. He turned his head so he could see the boy's face.

"I already said my goodbyes when they left the cottage this evening. I cried for them, and all I'm left with is the emptiness inside." The boy's face showed no emotion. It worried Wolf. All humans he had seen grieving and mourning showed some form of emotion. They cried, they were angry, they loved. This child didn't show any of these things.

"Thomas, you are unlike anyone I've ever seen. And I've seen many," Wolf said.

"Well, of course. How I came to be wasn't entirely natural. You know about the power. But do you really know how it works? I shouldn't exist, ask the one who gave you your fur. I also know that she wishes for me to live. She talks to me sometimes. If I let her."

Wolf looked up to the kid, slowing his pace, and using his keen senses. Thomas's eyes were different. They were silver with small blue specks. The specks were barely noticeable when he didn't look for them. Wolf now understood that whatever had given him this gift, it also altered his appearance slightly. He would tell his companions that other gifted humans might also have an abnormal appearance. He hadn't seen other humans with powers, but he had heard the rumors.

"There is another like you, someone with an unusual power. He doesn't have the same gift as you, but his family started like you. His ancestor passed down a gift of power. And with that, responsibility. They were different though. The Lady never speaks to him or his family. She understands his gift, but never explained it, as she will do with you. They had to find out

22

what it was, how to use it, and what the rules are." Wolf helped Thomas cross a fallen tree.

"You are more like us. You're an observer, but you can also act. We can act, but doing so would go against our mission. You'll never know if your interference led to that moment or not. That is what you share with your gifted cousins."

Thomas stopped walking. His eyes teared up, and he cried. Wolf didn't ask why he cried. He had a hunch.

Wolf kneeled down and cradled the boy with his tail. Thomas hid his face in the fur of the large animal.

When Thomas calmed down, he started talking through his sobs. "My sisters and brother. I'll never have cousins, nieces, or nephews. All my family is gone. Why did they have to take all of them? I couldn't change anything. You're right. I'll blame myself and wished to have gone with them. I don't want to be alone."

All Wolf did was hug the boy tighter and let him sob. The specks had disappeared from his irises and his speech had changed. This was the human behavior that Wolf expected from a grieving child.

When morning came, Wolf pushed his nose against Thomas's cheek. "Wake up, kid. I'll get you some food. Stay here." Wolf uncurled himself from the boy and looked for something edible. By the time he returned, Thomas had fallen back asleep.

As he woke up, tears filled his eyes again. He tried to stop, but he couldn't help it. When Wolf asked him what was wrong, the boy said he missed her; he missed all of them. He had a feeling he needed to go back, that they were still there. That it was all a bad dream. But it wasn't.

Wolf nudged him and licked away the tears. There wasn't

much else he could do for the boy. He was already doing everything he could—taking care of him and bringing him to the Lady. She would know what to do, she would take care of him.

Wolf carried a branch with berries to give to the kid and told him to climb on his back. The journey would be faster, and Thomas could take his time grieving. He told him he would take care of him as long as he needed it. With the boy on his back, he hurried towards the grove, the place where She was.

* * *

The forest became more dense as the unusual pair got closer towards the grove. As if the trees were trying to protect what was there. A Phoenix was flying high above the tree lines, looking down at the forest. They felt a disturbance and went on their way to find their companions. They thought of them as such, but they knew not all of them did. Their relationship was difficult to describe, and every time they talked about it, it ended in a disagreement. They knew the others were coming to heed the Lady's call, but they didn't see them yet. It was easy enough to hide, but none of them could mask their energy. No matter if they tried to hide themselves.

Phoenix returned to the clearing near the river. A small branch of the river led to a pond, just large enough for one of the companions.

"Any sign of them?" A soft voice spoke to Phoenix.

"No, nothing yet." The voice of Phoenix wasn't audible. Just like the others, they used telepathy to shape words inside the other's mind.

"They are getting closer. I can feel it," said the soft voice.

Slowly, a face appeared in the fog surrounding the grove. It was a young woman, not of flesh and blood. It was an ethereal appearance. Phoenix bowed towards her.

"It's good to see you again, Lady. It's been too long," said Phoenix raising their head.

The Lady walked towards Phoenix and put her hand on their head. Her hand didn't vanish through their body, but rested slightly on top. They felt a slight pressure where her hand was, but it was more of a sensation, no physical presence.

"I've missed you. I'm glad when we're all together. I wish you would visit me more often." She smiled genuinely.

"Lady, I don't follow days like living creatures. I don't think any of us knows how much time has passed since the last time we saw one another. That's why we're good at our job. We're here with a mission and not for companionship." Phoenix looked her in the eyes and saw sadness welling up.

"I know, but you're the only ones who I can talk with. If I communicate with others, it's intervening, and that's not something I'm supposed to do. Not for selfish reasons. Others were punished for it. I only wish you would tell me more about what's happening out there. I can't see everything."

"My Lady…" Phoenix bowed their head. "I'm sorry for not keeping you informed with everything going on. It's only since we've been here that we've got physical bodies and experience time to some degree. We've never reported to anyone other than our masters. Please don't misunderstand us. I'm grateful for what you've given us. I would never want to go back to what I was before, but we need time to adjust. It's only been a short while since I learned that living creatures started… Living, after all."

The Lady smiled at Phoenix as she lifted their head. "I don't accuse you of anything. Change is hard. Not just for you, but for anyone. Even me. It takes time, and time is something we both have. I'll be here, forever waiting for your return. I just hope you won't forget me."

The water in the creek moved as a gray fin slashed through the water.

"Hello, my dearest fellows. Long time no see. I notice I'm not the last to arrive, for once." Dolphin jumped out of the water to greet his friends. The Lady laughed, and Phoenix nodded slightly to Dolphin.

"Lady, I've missed you. I wish the waters here weren't as rough this far upstream. It took me a while to get past the new waterfall. Perhaps you can guide the water into a smoother path? Maybe I can visit you here more often, because I like it here. The beaches, cliffs, and ocean all look the same to me now. The deep inlands are so refreshing. I've seen a lot of new life in here and in the rivers. And new vegetations. I hope one day I can observe them properly." Dolphin kept talking about his adventures.

"I'll go see where the others are, my Lady," whispered Phoenix before they left. The Lady nodded slightly and kept listening to the Dolphin's stories. She could finally learn how life underwater was and what was happening near the coast. She rarely heard anything about it. The water flowed there and never returned.

* * *

Thomas needed to know how to survive by himself, Wolf thought. Wolf didn't know what would happen to the boy after

26

their meeting, and he felt a strange responsibility for him. He wanted Thomas to survive. Lady would base the decision on his and his companions' advice, and he knew that at least one would disagree with him.

Wolf wasn't looking forward to the meeting. He knew his companions would make this harder than it needed to be. Dolphin would be too excited. Fox was selfish enough to try to exploit the boy's powers. He didn't know the other two very well.

Phoenix would stay quiet, he thought, until they formed their opinion, and that opinion wouldn't change. Bear was a mystery to Wolf. She spent half her time sleeping instead of doing what she was supposed to do.

Thomas yawned. Wolf had given him small chores to keep his body occupied while his mind focused. He did well with his chores, gathering dry wood for a fire and picking berries. The crying wasn't as frequent anymore, although Wolf could still feel the boy's discomfort. He deserved an early night. Thomas cuddled up to Wolf, and he wrapped the boy with his tail to keep him warm.

* * *

The Lady meditated in the center of the clearing. She often did because it was the easiest way to connect with life. She felt the pulse, rhythmic and steady. Everything felt fine.

The only major disturbance was the explosion a few days ago. Wolf would tell her what happened. He was usually one of the quickest to arrive when she called but not this time. Something was keeping him. He was getting closer, although slowly, and he rested every night. That's unlike him, the Lady thought.

The Lady suspected he was bringing a human. It matched the patterns. It would be the first one she'd met in centuries. She was curious to see how they had evolved. It wasn't a good idea to show herself to humans; she learned the hard way. Although they were a loving species, they would often love so much it was tainted with jealousy and obsession. She hoped that one day they would learn moderation.

Nebula came back from her nightly hunting trip and took her place between the Lady's legs. The Lady was distracted, just for a bit, but soon found her focus again. Reading the energy of life like this calmed her mind. She felt connected to the ley lines. She still needed the five observers to tell her about what happened; the energy only conveyed a feeling, and she could only know if things were out of harmony. It wasn't her place to tell the world what to do or how to live; it was her job to keep the balance. She failed doing that last time, and she was determined not to fail again.

Phoenix landed in front of her. They stayed quiet out of respect for her and waited until she allowed them to speak. Nebula noticed the arrival of the grand bird and acknowledged it with a nod. Phoenix bowed their head to greet him back. They weren't fond of the feline, but it wasn't necessary for their job to be. The sun rose when the Lady opened her eyes again. She felt Nebula between her legs, and she stroked his dark blue fur.

"His fur is special. You might not have noticed it, but the silver spots on his fur change. They reflect the star patterns of this season. I don't know how it works exactly; it's wondrous." Nebula purred at the compliment and licked her finger playfully. "What is it you want to say, Phoenix?"

"They're almost here. Maybe a day or two, depending on

how fast they're traveling. There is one of us who needs a little convincing. I'll be leaving for the day to do so." Phoenix bowed and flew off again.

* * *

It was winter which meant the fifth of the companions would be sleeping. Phoenix didn't look forward to that encounter. Her mood was generally bad, but waking her from her winter sleep was terrifying. They knew where she preferred to hibernate. All of them found their favorite spots soon after they were free to roam. It flew towards the mountains in the east. The mountains were high, and snow never melted. She preferred the cold. Phoenix liked the warmer climates. They often rested in a tropical archipelago in the south-west. Humans didn't come there, so the development of the flora and fauna were untouched. They thought humans were ruining nature instead of adding to it. Their opinion didn't matter. They were an observer. And now it was time to embrace the cold and wake a very grumpy bear.

* * *

Thomas and Wolf woke up early that morning and set off. "Soon we'll be at our destination. I hope you're not afraid of the others. They appear as animals, but we're not," Wolf whispered.

"I don't know. I haven't seen many of them besides the ones close to our house and the livestock. You'll be with me, right? Then I'm sure I'll be okay." The boy had gotten used to walking while holding Wolf's fur. Wolf didn't mind. He noticed a significant change in confidence when he was touching his fur. The boy needed that confidence, especially at the meeting. He knew the others wouldn't be as kind to the boy as he was. He feared the boy would be on trial when the others found out about his gift. The boy didn't know how to control it, which made him a hazard. If he received training, he might abuse his power for his own gain depending on his true nature. Wolf hadn't seen selfish or self-centered attitude in the boy, but there was no way to predict how he would develop.

Thomas looked around for fruit, seeds, and mushrooms to eat. He was getting better at it. He recognized them more quickly and remembered which ones were ripe and which weren't. Wolf didn't eat them, but he had paid attention to other forest creatures when they were looking for food. As an observer he was knowledgeable, but that didn't make him a teacher. If Thomas didn't have any skill in foraging or cooking already, he would've been helpless. His parents did well in the initial education, but he needed more. It was an upside to a large family—everyone had to chip in. Even if his parents were still alive, the boy needed more teaching than they could provide.

At nightfall, Wolf saw the mountains looming in the east. They would arrive the next day. The Lady picked this grove so humans wouldn't come near. Wolf suspected Thomas was the first human to enter the clearing since his arrival.

"Tomorrow you'll have to ride on my back again. The forest will be thick with vegetation, and it'll be too difficult for you to walk. It'll also be faster. I hope you don't mind." Wolf laid down, and Thomas sat with his back against the giant beast.

"What will they do to me?" Thomas looked at him with concern in his eyes.

"They will question you about what happened and who you are. I'll make sure no harm will come to you. After the questions, we will decide what will happen. Your gift can be dangerous. People might hunt you down and force you to use it to their advantage. We have to be sure you're safe and that you're able to defend yourself from different kinds of threats. The Lady you'll meet has a gift, but she is not human. I'm sure she can teach you what you need to know, but someday you'll have to go back to live with other humans."

Wolf tried to comfort the boy. Lying wouldn't be right; the boy deserved the truth. No good came from lying when it concerned someone's future. He had been here long enough to have seen bad consequences. The boy needed to be prepared for all the good and bad he might encounter.

"My friends will be waiting there. They will know what to do. I hope you're ready to share your story for a second time," Wolf said.

"I hope so. Does that mean tomorrow will be our last day together?" Thomas looked at Wolf with watery eyes.

"I don't know." Wolf noticed the boy felt uneasy. The event had left its mark on the boy. Since he was inexperienced in the world, the loss of his family would infuse his gift. Wolf had noticed the differences between the real Thomas and his power. The boy's presence lessened during their brief period together. Whatever the Lady's plan was, it had to be done quickly. Soon all of Thomas would be gone.

"Go to sleep now. We will leave at dawn, and hopefully we'll arrive before noon. There is food and water where we're headed, so I hope you can hold out until then." Wolf wrapped his tail around the boy and pretended to go to sleep.

The boy buried himself into Wolf's fur for the last time. He fell asleep soon after, but his nights were restless. He had nightmares. The thick fur suppressed most of his screams, but Wolf felt them. He hoped that the boy could rest easily again after meeting the Lady.

* * *

Phoenix had to rely on their feeling to find the energy of Bear. All five of them could sense each other as long as they focused hard enough. Bear chose a cave near the peak of the highest mountain. "How convenient," Phoenix thought. Phoenix landed and hopped towards Bear. She was sleeping soundly. It would take her hours to fully awaken. Phoenix threw rocks at her, then they tried sounds. Nothing worked. Next the bird used their claws to trigger a pain reflex. One of the paws reacted and hit Phoenix. The bird became angry and used more force. Finally, Bear woke up and roared at the bird. She slashed with her front paws to protect herself from the unseen threat. Phoenix stayed back for their own safety. After Bear calmed down a little, Phoenix spoke to her.

"We have to go. The Lady is calling for us."

"Why? She knows it's winter." Bear yawned, her sharp teeth revealed.

"Something happened that has great consequences for the world. She needs our judgment. She needs all five." Phoenix hoped Bear noticed the urgency.

"Is everyone there yet?" Bear tried to stand on her feet and stretched, to get the blood flowing again.

"No, Wolf is the last to arrive, and he has a human with him. He will be on trial. We have to go now; they will arrive tomorrow."

Bear growled. She didn't like it, but she was loyal to the Lady. She couldn't let her down.

"Fine. I'll be there tomorrow. I have to find some food before I make the journey. I will be on time."

Phoenix nodded and flew off. They trusted the word of Bear. Throughout the years, she had proven herself as the most loyal and honest of all of them.

"Here they come," observed Phoenix. They flew down from a tall tree they had used as a lookout. They took their place next to the Lady. Dolphin swam in the pond nearby. Bear had just arrived, but took the opportunity to rest some more. Fox, who had arrived earlier that morning, hid in the bushes, still eating his last prey. Even when he didn't have to eat, his instincts caught up with him.

Wolf and the boy entered the grove. The boy's hair appeared almost white in the bright sun. He looked uncomfortable seeing a large brown bear, a bright-colored bird, and the ethereal appearance of a woman.

Wolf lowered his head and bowed to the Lady. "My Lady." The woman nodded in return. She walked towards the boy and lowered to see his face more clearly. "What's your name, young one?"

The boy stepped back and crossed his arms in front of his body. Wolf used his tail to keep the boy from walking back further.

"I'm sorry. I didn't mean to frighten you. I'm the Lady of the forest and these are my friends. Wolf brought you to me because I can help you." The Lady smiled and extended her hand.

The boy looked at Wolf for reassurance. He nodded, and the boy shook the Lady's hand. "My name is Thomas." He looked at her eyes. They weren't like other people's eyes. The irises moved. Little sparkles moved around like the shimmers in the nearby pond. A smile appeared on her face.

"Nice to meet you, Thomas. I'm truly sorry about what happened, and I wish I could have prevented it. I only noticed the danger of the powersink until its energy was released." The Lady hugged the boy but only just. She didn't expect him to hug her back. A moment later she felt the thin arms of the boy wrap around her neck and tears flowing on her shoulders.

Bear woke up from the cries and joined the others. Fox was still cautious and waited in the woods. He preferred being alone and was wary of others. Wolf could see him, but he knew the boy hadn't seen Fox.

The Lady made sure Thomas felt at ease. Before she asked more of him, she gave him water and food. Wolf was still watching over him and didn't leave his side. Phoenix noticed.

"Thomas, do you know why Wolf brought you here?" The Lady asked.

"He said you wanted to know what happened the night of the explosion." He looked down, focusing on peeling the fruit.

"Yes, that's correct. Will you tell me about it?" The Lady waited patiently for Thomas to start.

"I told them it would happen, but my parents didn't listen. I was sick, and they didn't take me to the meeting. The whole village was there when the barn exploded." He talked fast, as if he wanted to get it over with.

"I'm sorry. I honestly wish I could have prevented it. How did you know it was going to happen?"

"I saw it happen. When I close my eyes, I see dreams, but lately these dreams have started coming true."

"Are you asleep when that happens?"

34

"No, only the dreams I see when I'm awake come true," the boy said.

Wolf was glad to hear this, because he didn't want the nightmares Thomas had had the past few days to come true.

"Your parents didn't believe you when you said something bad would happen?"

"I have six brothers and sisters. Had… It was always chaos, and they didn't have much time for me. My two younger sisters took up most of their time. I don't know if they didn't hear my warnings, or that they thought the dreams were part of my sickness." He kept fidgeting with his fingers to distract himself from the nerves.

"I'm sure they would've believed you if you had time to explain everything. Have other things happened around you, besides the dreams?"

"My older brother often called me weird. Animals always came to me, not him. I also found more food and fossils than he did."

"You weren't just lucky?"

"No, I can attest to that. He's able to feed himself with fruits and roots. I didn't have to teach him much. He even knows the difference between edible and poisonous ones," Wolf said.

"Can you explain how you know this, Thomas?"

"I don't know. I just feel which ones are good and which ones are bad. They feel different."

"Is that why you went with Wolf as well? Because you knew he was good?"

"Yes. I felt I should go with him. I didn't know what else to do."

"I see. What do you feel around me?"

"The same thing I felt from my mom." This was the first time he looked toward the Lady, but he still didn't make eye contact.

"Then I know she loved you very much."

Thomas nodded and pointed at Bear.

"She also feels like that. The bird doesn't feel like anything. In the water I feel another good one."

Dolphin jumped out of the water in joy. While he kept quiet, the boy noticed him, and that made him happy.

"There's another one in the forest, but he doesn't feel as good."

That remark surprised everyone. None of them knew that the boy had noticed Fox. Fox came into the clearing and sat down next to Bear, but said nothing. Instead, he started cleaning his fur.

"You definitely have a gift, Thomas. You knew he was there, even though you couldn't see him?"

Thomas nodded.

"Would you like to stay here for a while? Until we know what your gift is." The Lady smiled at him.

Thomas looked at Wolf. "I would like that."

* * *

That night Thomas fell asleep against Wolf, like he did the night before. Phoenix landed beside the duo.

"Don't get too attached to him. It's not good. You have your own duties." There were no emotions in their speech or face that Wolf could recognize.

"Right now, this boy is my duty. You have no idea what he can do, even I have only seen a glimpse of his true abilities. I think it's our responsibility to make sure Thomas is safe and that he's properly educated so he won't become a danger." He knew his attachment was more than he dared to admit.

"You know more about this gift, something the boy himself doesn't know."

"I do." Wolf wasn't sure if it was wise to share this information without the others present, but he needed to share it with someone. "When his gift is dominant, the boy's personality will change. He isn't Thomas anymore. I haven't spoken much when he's in that state, but then he will look at things rationally. As if he's devoid of emotion. The things he knows then, also don't reflect that of a normal nine-year-old child." Wolf felt his anger rise. He knew that Phoenix was fishing for information it could use against him.

"Might this, other personality, become a danger to us or the Lady?" Phoenix emphasized danger. Wolf knew what Phoenix was doing.

"Like I said, he needs proper education and guidance. Then we make sure that both of them, the gift and the boy, won't be a threat."

"Are they now?" Phoenix looked away.

"I don't believe so. I suspect his gift holds more than he knows now."

"Wouldn't it be better if he never learned to use his gift in the first place?" Phoenix made their words sound casual, but their tone betrayed it.

"Don't underestimate him or the gift. He will know eventually." Wolf squinted.

Phoenix moved closer to Wolf with an intense stare. "I mean, get rid of him."

"We can't interfere." Wolf's ears were upright, the hair on his back rising.

"And guiding him isn't interfering?" Phoenix moved back.

"That's different," Wolf said, but he wasn't convinced by his words. The Lady overheard what Phoenix had suggested and joined them.

"Educating him about his gift will be as much interfering as telling an otter how to swim. They will learn to swim even when they're alone. We will just speed up the process to mastery. I agree with Wolf that Thomas should be educated. I'm also very curious as to why Thomas has this gift and what he's capable of. If you don't like it, you won't have to partake." It seemed like the Lady had already decided what was going to happen with the boy.

Phoenix didn't say anything.

"I know about your obsession with death, but this boy won't come back once his heart stops beating. You won't be just an observer anymore, should you kill him. I won't let you." Wolf warned them.

"You won't? Wouldn't that be interfering as well?" Phoenix said.

"I'm an observer here; my companions are not part of this ecosystem and are excluded. I can take you on if I have to. I'm with the Lady, her vote outweighs ours," Wolf said.

"Phoenix, I know what you want to do, but it's not right. His birth wasn't an accident, and more people will be born with gifts. I want to know why and how they work. The gifts are part of this world. We can't just eliminate every dangerous thing. Look at the cycle of life; danger is everywhere. Let's just hope Thomas won't be the dangerous one." The Lady wondered if she was the one who gave this gift to the boy, but she didn't quite remember.

Phoenix accepted that their solution wasn't viable and retreated for the night.

The Lady stayed with Thomas and Wolf a little longer.

"Such a young thing but already lost everyone he knew and loved. I hope we can give him a home. Will you take him for a walk tomorrow? I have to talk with Fox, Dolphin, and Bear. Things will be difficult if the others agree with Phoenix." She kissed Thomas on his forehead before disappearing into the night.

Wolf knew what she meant. If the majority of them thought Thomas was a potential danger, the Lady had to consider it.

* * *

The next morning, Thomas washed his face in the pond. Dolphin blew water out of his blowhole to entertain the boy. Thomas laughed for the first time since the explosion.

"Hello there, little one. We haven't met yet. Your name is Thomas, is it not?"

"Yes, that's me. What are you?" Thomas looked at the blue gray creature with curious eyes.

"I'm a... The Lady has granted me the honor of being a dolphin. We live in the ocean most of the time, and we eat fish. Do you like fish?" Dolphin swam a quick lap around the pond.

"I do, but we didn't eat it often, since we live so far away from the coast. My father didn't have the time to go fishing himself."

"Today you will eat fish. I'll make sure of that," Dolphin whistled.

"Maybe you could catch some for me as well? I'm still hungry." Bear walked over with a yawn. She drank some water and laid down again.

"I could fish the entire ocean and you'd still be hungry, my dear."

39

"That's not… untrue. I should still be sleeping right now." Another yawn escaped her.

"I'm sorry." Thomas looked at his feet; his smile disappeared.

"It's not your fault, hun. You couldn't have seen it happen. Well, you did. But you couldn't do anything to stop it, right?" Bear tried to comfort him.

"N-no, I guess not."

"How often do you see dreams of the future?" Dolphin asked.

"Two or three times a day." Thomas sat down at the edge of the pond and took off his shoes. His toes touched the water. A shiver went from his toes to his head.

"Have you seen us in those dreams?" Bear asked curiously.

Thomas had to think before he answered. There had been so many, but each of these creatures differed from normal dolphins, bears, foxes, and wolves. "No. Even Wolf wasn't in them."

"So you see things about events happening around you." Dolphin was playing in the water while listening to the two talking.

"Most of the times the things I see happen far away. I don't know the places, but some come back more often than others." Thomas kicked the water towards Dolphin who tried to catch the water mid-air.

"What do you do when you see those things?" Bear was still tired and settled on the grass.

"Nothing. I can't do anything about it if it happens. I pretend it's a dream I have at night."

"You're smart for your age. Most humans I see think little about anything. Consequences seem nonexistent. But you do see them, don't you?" Dolphin scattered as it jumped out of the water with a somersault.

"What do you mean, consequences?" Thomas looked up confused.

"When you do one thing, another thing happens. Like when you throw a rock into the water, ripples will appear. Your actions will cause someone or something to react. Sometimes the consequences of one's actions are good or bad. Humans don't consider consequences beyond the first ripple, or they act regardless of the outcome." Dolphin tried to explain.

"Why would people do something that's bad?" Thomas thought hard, but he couldn't think of anything.

"I don't know, I can only tell you what I've seen. You said you had brothers and sisters. Weren't they ever punished by your parents?"

Thomas thought about his family and tears appeared in his eyes.

Bear shook her head at Dolphin.

Wolf approached them and nodded to his companions.

"Thomas, will you come with me? We should gather food for you." He asked.

The Lady appeared when Wolf and Thomas left and sat beside Bear. Fox joined them shortly after to start the discussion about Thomas.

Dolphin and Bear were convinced that Thomas was no danger and educating him would help. Fox, who didn't hear everything being said the previous day, remained neutral. He thought humans were unpredictable and that even if Thomas wasn't a danger now, that was no guarantee of who he would be in the future. Keeping the boy in sight was the best way to make sure he wouldn't become a danger to the planet.

When Thomas and Wolf came back, the others were waiting.

"Thomas, you shall stay with me. Together we will figure out how you can control the dreams." The Lady smiled and opened her arms for a hug.

Thomas ran to her and fell into her embrace. He thought of his mother when he felt her warmth.

The witch of Monterra Mountain

On the mountainside of Monterra, there was a village at the edge of the forest. It was cold, but the mountain was generous with wood, coal, and ore. Many blacksmiths trained in these regions because of this. Some of the best tools came from this region, and swordsmen came here especially to commission a sword.

Many people traveled through the region — not just swordsmen or blacksmith apprentices, but also merchants who came to buy metal tools to sell in villages farther away from the mountains. It was the merchants who passed on stories and messages between villages, and they often told the story about this particular area of the Monterra mountains, the North regions, a story of a witch.

A woman lived deep in the mountains, in a place where snow was eternal. No one knew how old she was. Everyone who saw her thought she was the most beautiful woman alive, even the married men who were deeply in love with their wives. Her description changed with each person who saw her. Some said her hair was white as snow; others had seen her with raven black hair. For a while people thought there were two women, maybe even twins. Her skin looked like marble, clear and brittle, without any marks and her lips pink like a cherry's blossom. Women hated her. Men adored her. Although neither really knew her or could explain why they felt this way.

The mountaintops didn't provide for everything the woman needed, so sometimes she came down to the nearest village for supplies. The grocer, traveling merchants at the inn, and the blacksmith were the only people she ever visited. Throughout the years her appearance never changed, except for her hair. Once, forced to spend the night at the inn as bad weather prevented her from returning home, her hair had changed color overnight. That's when everyone started calling her a witch, although no one had seen how she did it. Young girls would use lemon juice to bleach their hair in summer, but that took days before the change was visible. They couldn't explain how the woman had changed her hair's color in such a short time, so they labeled it magic.

What the villagers didn't know was that she was a real witch, although she'd never used magic to change the color of her hair. She rarely used magic at all. There was no need for it.

She lived a regular human life, doing all her daily chores without magic. The only time she used magic was when she imbued potions at the request of villagers. The blacksmith and the grocer passed on the requests in secret. None of the villagers wanted others to know that they needed the witch's help.

Most of the villagers were afraid of her. They thought her unpredictable; they didn't know how strong her powers were or what she could do with them. It was the fear of the unknown and no willingness to find out.

The blacksmith and grocer came to know her through her frequent visits and liked her more with each visit. They shared a bond of trust and respect the witch didn't have with anyone else.

One day the witch came down from the mountain shortly after a new young man had come into town. He worked as the blacksmith's apprentice until he was good enough to forge his own sword and kill a bear with it. That would be proof of his skill in the craft. People would trust his work and his strength.

The witch visited her usual stops for supplies, and when she came to the blacksmith's workplace, the apprentice approached her. The blacksmith was in the back and had not heard her coming in. She saw the young man and instantly fell in love with his bright smile. Under her hood, her hair turned white. He greeted the witch and asked what he could do for her. She couldn't help smiling back and introduced herself as the blacksmith came back in and rushed to take care of this valuable customer. When she left, the blacksmith told his apprentice who she was. He shrugged and said he liked her. City life had taught him many things, and one of those things was to follow his gut feeling. Gossip was for old ladies looking for something to occupy their time.

Months went by with small flirtations from both sides. None of this affection went unnoticed by the other girls in the village who desperately tried to make the young man theirs. Mothers tried to set him up with their daughters, but he was honest and kept the promise he had made to his mother: to not choose a wife until he was a full-fledged blacksmith. Only then would he be able to provide for her, and it would reveal whether the girl had the patience to wait for him. Such a display of respect and devotion would prove her affection for him to be genuine.

Slowly he grew older and people thought he didn't want to get married. Even the blacksmith, his mentor, thought he wasn't serious about his future anymore. The young apprentice was good, but he messed up his swords on purpose so he didn't have to fight the bear. The blacksmith taught him how to use the sword. He thought it might be his lack of confidence that made him not want to face the bear.

In truth, his fear was to express his feelings. He knew what everyone thought of the one he loved, and she'd never told him her age. In those rare moments they spent completely alone, she shared some secrets. For one, she showed how her hair changes color. The hood of her cape allowed her to hide her hair, but sometimes someone managed to catch a glimpse of her hair. It was usually black, but positive emotions could turn it white. She had no control over it unlike her other magic.

The apprentice tucked a strand of hair behind her ear. He liked how it shined, no matter if it was white or black, she looked beautiful with both.

The witch asked why he hadn't killed a bear yet, even though he could do it. His strength was obvious from his muscular chest, and his knives were requested often. He was ready for independence. She knew he needed to get on with his life, with or without her, but she never told him she cared for him.

Finally, after a long talk, she had persuaded him. He would forge his best sword yet and slay a bear. A few months later he left the blacksmith's home and went off into the forest. The sword he'd crafted was sharp enough to cut leaves in half mid-air. The time he'd chosen for this confrontation proved unfortunate. He came across a bear who had just given birth to a cub and in her defensive rage she mauled the apprentice. He stumbled over a tree's root and his sword fell. Before he could reach it, the bear was already towering over him. She raised her paw again and knocked him out.

Hours later the witch came down into the forest to see how he fared. She felt the bear's emotions and knew something was wrong. When she found the young man he was near death. After the bear struck him, he had fallen and hit his head against a rock. His consciousness had left him as blood streamed from his head wound. She cried for the first time in her life. Her sobs could be heard throughout the whole forest. In her weakest moment she recalled a spell she had learned many years ago to heal animals. She wasn't certain it would work on humans, but she had to try. After her spell the bleeding stopped, but he was still unconscious. It would take time before he would wake up again. She made a fire and laid down next to him to keep him warm.

The young man woke up the next morning with a terrible headache and the beautiful woman laying beside him. He kissed her cheek, grabbed his sword and ran off into the forest to finish his mission and keep his promise. He didn't want to leave her alone, but he knew she would be safe. She always had a knife hidden in her boot to cut herbs she'd find on her way back home, but it was sharp enough to injure or kill.

The witch woke up to find the apprentice gone. She ran through the forest to the village, hoping he would've gone home instead of doing something stupid. The blacksmith's house was empty when she checked it. After a few minutes of walking through the village, she heard laughter from the inn. She looked through the window and saw him standing in the middle of the crowd, slightly taller than the rest. The witch opened the door and everyone looked at her. The man smiled wide and threw his arms up in the air. He announced that she was the woman he would give his life to, now that he was a real blacksmith. Behind the man did not lay the body of a bear but of a wolf. He said he couldn't kill a bear with a cub. Being left as an orphan was the worst thing that could happen to a child. The villagers asked him repeatedly if his choice for his life partner was the right one. He responded with a question of his own and asked the villagers if his choice of not killing the mother bear was the right one. All agreed. He explained he didn't want his child to grow up without a father either as he winked at the witch. She blushed slightly and turned her head away from the crowd. It was a lie, but that was the only reason the villagers accepted his choice and a few other women congratulated her reluctantly. They were jealous an outsider stole away a good man. The man laughed and put his arm around his future wife. They left the inn together, leaving the villagers speechless.

The new blacksmith stayed with the witch and kept working with his mentor. It didn't take long for the witch to get pregnant, and the blacksmith's wish for a baby girl was granted. He always wondered if it was a coincidence, or if his wife's magic made his wish come true.

Shepherd's stick

A man, curious about life and the world, was once asked by a child about what lies beyond the desert. The man, the scholar of his village, didn't know but told the child he would find out. In all his life, he had never asked that question. His curiosity had started with questioning the things he knew and saw, but he was mostly interested in the 'why' of things, rather than what it was. The child, young as he was, questioned everything he didn't know or hadn't seen. The man envied the child for this boundless curiosity, not limited by what he saw. They spoke together regularly, wondering about the world, but the child kept asking about the desert. The man promised the child he would look into what lay beyond it.

He researched his books but found nothing. The ancestors of their tribe never wandered beyond their village's borders, and the tales of merchants couldn't be trusted. Their stories never made it into the journals of the tribesmen. There was only one mention about the desert in all the books in the village: the desert is dangerous and cursed. The writer warned to stay away. The borders around the village were created with this reason in mind. The scholar withheld this from the child, so he wouldn't be scared.

A few years later another child asked him about the desert, and he still couldn't answer. Most of the questions from his pupils were about the village or something close to them. Rarely anyone, even adults, asked about the desert. The only tales he knew were used to scare children. Ghost stories about gods and curses. People grew up with these stories and had accepted that the desert was something to avoid.

The man went to look for himself to see if these stories were true. He didn't know them as anything other than a bedtime story, if there was any truth in them. If he couldn't find it in their history, he would write about the desert himself. He'd never heard of anyone being attacked, and merchants often came to their village, some even several times a year, so there had to be a way to travel through the desert. He asked one of them how they reached the village, and the merchant told him he found his way through the desert. There were paths made by and for people who travel the sands. They warned him not to go into the desert alone. One wrong step could be fatal, if you didn't know where to go. And not just because of the snakes and scorpions.

The scholar didn't know what to expect, apart from a lot of sand and a few oases. The merchant's warning was etched in his mind, as was the warning by his ancestor. He knew people used to live in the desert a long time ago, but he knew nothing else. A few merchants mentioned ruins as they journeyed through the desert. Some found skeletons that could have been fellow merchants but might have lain there for centuries. Because of the shifting sands it was impossible to know for certain.

He wrote all the stories and warnings down in a book he would take with him. Then he could check off which stories were true and which were false.

The desert ruins were old. There was one merchant brave enough to examine a pillar he came across. It contained symbols, but most of them were faded. He didn't recognize them from anything he'd seen before. His inspection didn't last long; a dozen snakes came crawling around the pillar as if to protect it. It was just a small one at first, but soon dozens of smaller snakes and a big one were hiding in the bushes surrounding the pillar. The large snake curled around the pillar to cover up the view from the merchant. He wasn't afraid of snakes, but this one didn't look familiar. He didn't know how venomous it was. The large snake bit the merchant as he touched a part of the pillar, and he died minutes after. A merchant who came to the oasis later, found a few lines scribbled on an old piece of parchment next to the corpse. The first merchant wrote it while the venom was spreading through his body. He pinned the warning on a palm tree in the nearest oasis.

This was just one of the many stories that merchants told everyone as a warning before going into the desert, but people stopped asking about the dangers. The warning was enough for people to avoid the desert, but they welcomed everyone who braved the desert. The villagers were friendly but superstitious.

Most of the knowledge of the desert came from merchants and while they were welcome, the villagers still didn't trust them enough to take their words for truth. They accepted the warnings since it confirmed the danger they already believed in, but the stories revealed nothing about what caused these dangers. Was it really just the environment, or was there something else going on?

The scholar's journey into the desert would take away some of that superstition. This could only benefit the tribe. He wanted to know whether the merchant's stories were true, or whether they had lied. What if the merchants wanted to keep the villagers from entering the desert? He knew a few merchants had attempted to find a huge treasure, deep within the desert, but they left after seeing ghosts. The treasure might be the reason they wanted to keep people away.

The scholar wasn't afraid of ghosts, knowing they couldn't hurt him. But it was really the desert itself he feared—the scorching heat and the lack of water. One merchant told him he should cover up his whole body, keeping his body temperature up, instead of cool. By keeping warm, the warmth of the desert wouldn't affect him as much. The clothing would also protect him from exposure to the sun. Underneath his robe, he carried a few tools, a hatchet, and as many sheepskins with water as he could carry without it becoming a burden.

The scholar prepared for several weeks. He left his wife and son and told his brother to take care of them while he was away. His wife begged him to stay and go on his journey when his son was a man of his own. The night before he was to leave, she'd dreamed he would never come back. The merchant's tales added to her fear of losing her husband, and she couldn't stand the thought of their son growing up without a father.

Her brother-in-law had his own family to care for, and she doubted he would want another two mouths to feed. The scholar pressed enough money in her hand to feed them for a year and promised to be back before the money ran out. He also gave her his mother's ring. He told her that the white gem would turn red if anything happened to him. That's what his father had told his mother every day when he went to work in the fields near the desert.

He left before sunrise. He kissed his wife goodbye and left his necklace in his son's hand. A merchant would show him the way to the merchant paths. Halfway through the fields the merchant stopped and explained the rest of the way into the desert. All he had to do was to follow this path and keep following the sun until the first marker, a long pole stuck in the sand. It was high enough to still be visible even after a sandstorm. The markers would show him the rest of the way. The merchant went toward the mountains instead of deeper into the desert. It was a place few people came.

The fields closest to the desert were the domain of the shepherds. The sheep and goats liked to eat the grass that grew there, nothing else would take root. One shepherd gave him a walking stick as he passed the meadow. The shepherd said he would need it. At first the scholar declined. The shepherd looked old and fragile, so surely he would need it more. The shepherd assured the man he could walk through the desert and back without getting tired. He demonstrated his vitality with a small dance. The man smiled at the display, took the stick gratefully, and walked on into the desert. The first few days weren't any harder than he'd expected, he reached the first oasis without too much trouble. The heat during the day and the cold during the night took some getting used to, but it wasn't something he couldn't handle. The only difference between here and his village was the shade.

He was in luck. A merchant had stopped at the first oasis, so he bought more food for the rest of his journey. The merchant shared his tales and the location of another oasis. That was the farthest the merchant had gone, because it wasn't necessary to travel far into the desert when he traveled between the mountains and the desert village. The man thanked him and left the next morning, after refilling his sheepskins with water from the oasis. With the new directions, the man found the second oasis with little trouble.

At the next oasis all he found was a small chest half buried on the shore of the oasis. The man opened it and found some papers. There were warnings and dates written on the pages. Other adventurers had tried to cross the desert and had written down the dates and days they had walked beyond that point, to keep a log for themselves and others. No one had managed to spend more than four days out there. One had written that he found an oasis, but couldn't reach it. He claimed there was a mysterious force preventing him from reaching it.

He copied the pages and the general directions he followed to get here in his journal, carefully keeping track of everything he saw, heard, and read. He spent a day planning his actions. He knew he would be back after four days. He decided to take multiple trips to confirm the stories they told him.

After he left, and the oasis well out of sight, he felt something. It was a strange freezing sensation that made little sense in the blazing heat. At night he found out what it was. The merchant he'd talked to was right about the ghosts of the desert. When he lit a fire, the light revealed the blue lining of a man which slowly became more solid. The ghost stared at the man, expecting something. He still looked human, almost his age, but dressed differently. A style he didn't recognize.

The man expected ghosts because of the multitude of stories that confirmed their presence. He greeted the ghost. Being polite would at least delay his death if this ghost was seeking revenge, as most stories suggested. To the man's surprise, the ghost talked back.

The ghost told the man about a treasure. A grand treasure left behind by an extinct civilization. They'd all died, although the ghost couldn't say how or why. The ghost was even willing to show him the way. After a few hours, the ghost disappeared, but another took his place, this time a female ghost. She warned the man he would be tricked. That was all she said before she disappeared. The next morning, the man heard the voice of the male ghost who had kept him company during dinner. He'd reappeared to lead the way. The man was ready and grabbed his walking stick, asking the ghost to take the lead. The moment that the ghost turned around and saw the walking stick, he disappeared.

Confused by the sudden disappearance, the scholar set out in the direction the ghost had indicated. The next evening another ghost turned up, warning him to watch out for the other ghost. This one looked much younger, the same age as the female ghost. At the sight of his walking stick, this ghost also vanished and never returned. On the third night, the female ghost returned and asked him to turn around and go back to the world of the living. Before she could leave, he asked her about the walking stick. She looked, gasped, and disappeared.

The man decided he should at least stick to the four nights out before heading back. He moved on, and on the fourth night the female ghost returned, but not alone. She had brought an elder. She said they should talk about what had happened to the man the past few days. The man showed his walking stick to the elder ghost. The elder didn't disappear like the rest, but was very interested.

He had heard of a story, back when he was still alive. It was a prophecy that the king's staff would return to set his people free. This walking stick was the king's staff. The ghost was lost in thought for a while, trying to recall the prophecy. The man asked about the treasure and why a king with such a vast treasure would use an ordinary stick as a staff. The elder said the king valued some things more than gold and jewels. This stick was from the very tree he used to play in as a child, and under which he had buried his mother when he was twelve years old. It had sentimental value, worth more than all the gold in the world. But it would only be worth that much to one person.

The scholar disagreed. There were at least three men that valued this stick. The king, obviously. The shepherd, who had used it daily with much pleasure as it made his job easier. And lastly, the scholar himself. The stick had brought him this far on his quest, and the man didn't know what would've happened if he had followed the ghosts. He was grateful for the staff. The elder ghost told him he would likely have ended up dead and in the same predicament as the ghosts: obsessed with what's hidden in the sands and bound to it.

The man told the elder of his quest for knowledge rather than treasure. The elder ghost nodded and said that must have been the reason the shepherd gave him the walking stick. The elder explained that he knew the shepherd. He was the one who cursed the sands to misguide all treasure hunters. The female ghost was one of the few good ones, one who would warn an honest traveler. She was a seer back in her time—a seer of people. She knew when someone lied and what was in their heart. Only good people heeded her warning and turned back. All greedy and selfish people pushed on, died, and became ghosts themselves. The elder apologized for calling the man selfish, for his quest was not one based on selfishness or greed, but curiosity. This was the only reason the scholar was still here, alive, and sane and the reason he would be allowed back if he wished.

The man, however, was intrigued by the prophecy of the king's staff. How could a stick, or staff, free the king's people? Were they held captive? By whom? The elder told the man to go back to the oasis, to gather more supplies, and wait for his appearance. He would then guide him to the ruins of the palace. The ghost needed time to think about what the man's appearance meant for him and his people.

The elder ghost didn't return for several days. When he finally appeared on the sixth day, he apologized. He hadn't realized how many days had passed because for a ghost time flowed differently. The ghost led the way through the sands, but they took a very different path than the first time. The man thought he was being led back towards the first oasis. But after five days, they arrived at a different oasis. The ghost told him that this was the last stop before the capital of his old country. No one had been to this oasis for centuries. The other ghosts made sure of that. The man asked the elder ghost about the pressure he'd felt when they entered the oasis. The elder replied that this area was spelled to keep enemies from finding their way to the capital. Only people who were invited would be allowed to the gates. They had to cross the boundaries of the old country that other people couldn't see or pass.

Five days after leaving the oasis, they arrived at the ruins of the old city. The towers of the palace stood tall in the sands, with the rest of the city buried in the surrounding sands. The ghost told the man to find a way to enter the palace. There were large towers at the corners of the ruin. The windows in those towers were his best shot of getting inside. The sands were blown high enough to reach them, and he hoped the inside of the palace wasn't filled with sand.

The ghost disappeared without giving him any directions to where inside the palace he ought to be. It took the man hours to find a window through which he could enter the palace. As soon as he put his foot down, another ghost appeared. It was the grand vizier of the kingdom.

The elder ghost whispered into the man's ear that the vizier could not be trusted and that he is the one who kept their people under a spell. The grand vizier told the man something different. The king's greed got out of hand and they punished his people for it. It was true he kept the people under a spell, including himself, but the king was the reason for all of it. The king had stolen an ancient artifact from the gods and asked his grand vizier to spell the artifact so no one could take it from him, especially the gods. The grand vizier warned the king about the consequences of such a spell. For mortals to defy a god was unspeakable. But the king's command was absolute. The vizier had cast his spell and felt the vibration of the earth change. They had angered the gods.

When the god came to claim what was rightfully his, he

threatened to eat every citizen, one by one, until the king would return the artifact. The vizier had prepared for this and knew the wrath of the gods couldn't be stopped, except through payment with death. He cursed the entire country's citizens to live as ghosts until someday someone could break the spell and reforge their bond of trust with the gods.

The king, having lost his life and his treasures, sent his most trusted adviser, his old grandfather, out as a ghost to bring back the one thing that could break the spell. It was said only a person in the god's good graces could do it and return the artifact to its rightful owner. The stick, said the grand vizier, was made of elderberry wood. The only tree as old as the gods themselves. It had the power to undo what had been done. Not just this spell, but more than that. The grand vizier begged the man to break the staff and burn it. Then the world would be safe from the gods' power.

The man listened to both sides of the story before picking a side. The ghosts couldn't hurt him, only manipulate his mind, which he was used to by now. The children he taught were also full of lies, blaming each other for the things they did. It had taught him how to recognize the truth, even if both parties failed to tell it. The man left without doing anything. He didn't want to anger the gods nor send their wrath upon people who didn't deserve it. He wrote the whole story down so he could study it. He would go back some day and help the ghosts.

   He returned home to his wife and son and hugged them tight. He buried the staff beneath his house and refrained from telling anyone what exactly happened during his journey. Ghosts, curses, and angry gods weren't good for morale in the village.

He confirmed to anyone who asked about the desert that the presence of ghosts and the heat of the sun would turn a man mad.

Later he tried to find the shepherd who had given him the walking stick, but he didn't work in the pasture anymore. He asked around town, and no one seemed to remember there ever being a shepherd. The ghosts still haunt the desert, and the ruins lay forgotten in the sands. Sometimes the man saw the grand vizier in his dreams, asking him to take action.

Years later, when his son was coming of age, the man told him the full story and asked what the young man would do. His son said he would seek out the god and ask for his story, because he didn't know his perspective. Maybe both ghosts were lying, but neither story changed the fact that the artifact was stolen and should be returned to its rightful owner. His son asked him if this story was another hypothetical situation to test his judgment. The man shook his head and told him this story was real.

The man thanked his son for opening his eyes. He had taught his son well, and he knew it wouldn't be long for him to be the student and his son the teacher. One day he would pick up the walking stick again and follow his son's advice. To seek out the god and make things right.

Archipelago of wonder

There once was a fisherman. He lived in a small village by the sea where he spent most of his time outside. Fishing was his occupation, but he often helped with construction and knew woodworking just as well. He even built a house on the waterside for his wife after they married. He wanted her to wake up with the sight of the sunrise over the sea. Every morning he left to catch enough fish to feed his family and sell some at the market.

His wife dried the fish, so they wouldn't spoil as fast. They considered her dried fish the best in the village. Fall was her busiest season since other fishermen brought their catch to her as well, to prepare for winter time.

The couple was working harder, and it showed. Lines creased their tanned faces, and their hands were rough. The fisherman's wife called the lines on her husband's face 'lines of love'. They were proof of what he was willing to do for the ones he loves.

One day the fisher was out at sea and a storm approached. It wasn't a big storm, but the timing of it couldn't be worse. He was out in the water where the bigger fish lived, and the waves had pushed him far out into the open sea — much farther than he had ever gone before. The fisherman took shelter under a sail and waited for the storm to pass.

After the storm cleared, he saw it damaged the boat, and it was taking in water. It was impossible to reach the village with the state the boat was in. He would sink before reaching the shore. He looked around to find something to fix the boat for long enough to get him safely ashore.

The fisherman heard water splashing, and he noticed a fin appear in the water. A dolphin tried to get his attention by spitting water in the air. A few miles away, barely visible, he saw land. It turned out to be a few small islands grouped together. He plugged the biggest hole with some rags and hoped it would keep long enough as he set sail for the islands.

The island's beach was white and sandy, and the water between the islands was clearer than the fisher had ever seen. It looked like paradise. It was much warmer than he was used to, and there were bright flowers between the trees he had never seen before. It seemed he could survive for a couple of days and repair his boat, if he could find enough food. He took out his axe and knife. The axe wasn't made for chopping trees, but it would have to do. He normally used the knife to cut the fishing lines when he caught a stubborn fish strong enough to pull him under. The first thing he had to do was find drinking water, food, and shelter. If the storm last night was any indication, the weather could turn from clear sky to winds and lightning strong enough to destroy his village in a second.

The fisher pulled his boat ashore as far as he could and locked it in with some logs he found near the forest's edge so it couldn't drift back into the ocean. Noises came from the forest when he collected the logs. That would be his next mission — seeing where those noises came from. Perhaps there were others on the island, and maybe they could help him. It sounded like music, but he wasn't certain. It could have been a bird. He slowly made his way through the forest, listening for the sounds he had heard earlier. The forest became thicker and thicker the further he went in. Small lizards crawled on the trees and birds jumped from branch to branch.

After an hour of walking and having no idea where he was or where he was going, he heard running water; it turned out to be a small creek. He tasted it, then drank some more. He filled his flask to be sure he had enough for the coming hours. The man followed the creek. If people lived on this island, they would need water. They would come here. Some birds picked at bright red berries, which meant they were safe to eat. He sliced one open and took a few with him for later. He found fruit trees growing next to the creek which provided him with food.

Night fell and the fisher still hadn't found another human or a hideout to spend the night. He thought it would be safer to sleep in a tree to keep most animals away. He didn't know if there were dangerous animals, but the leaves of the trees were big enough to provide him shelter from rain. It wasn't very comfortable, but the entire experience tired him enough to fall asleep.

A whisper woke him up. It sounded warm, soothing, and very close. Someone was calling him. Maybe the storm was a dream, and he was at home with his wife. The island must have been a dream. He opened his eyes and saw something sparkling in front of him. He was certain he was still dreaming. The sparkling thing whispered his name and asked him to open his eyes. He did and saw the voice belonged to a tiny human. With wings. The little woman had long flowing hair the color of the moon's reflection. Her eyes were as blue as the sea. Her figure was slim, and her skin reflected the light. She smiled at him. It was enough to enchant him. A warm blanket of comfort fell over him as he she whispered in his ear. She was beautiful. Even more beautiful than his own wife, he fell in love.

The love he felt was different from what the fisher felt for his wife. It was pure, almost like what he would feel for his own babe. Her mere presence was enough to make him happy. She smiled again and asked if he was lost. He nodded, and she held out her hand. Her touch revealed a village. It was filled with more of her kind. All of them had different colored hair, skin, and wings, but they were every bit as beautiful as her. The fisher was enchanted and asked her what she was. "A nymph," she said. "We don't have many human visitors, but it's our duty to maintain the balance of these islands. You cannot stay here as that would upset the guardians. We can help you get back to your home. We'll repair your boat and give you provisions for the journey back."

The nymphs kept their word. A few days later the boat was repaired and filled with enough provisions to make the journey home. Saying goodbye was painful for the fisher. He knew he wouldn't see his new friend ever again. He told her he would never be happy again if they weren't together. The nymph felt the same way. She was an outsider in the village. Bringing a human into their village was only the latest of incidents. The elders thought her mind was too different. The humanity of the fisher had touched her, she thought it was beautiful. The nymph told the fisher to close his eyes. He felt a warm sensation close to his heart. It was the same sensation he felt when his wife first smiled at him and when they married. He opened his eyes, and she was gone. He held his hand over his heart where he still felt the warmth.

Once back at sea he pinched himself to make sure he was truly awake. His adventures on the islands had been short, but they had left a deep impression. He would never forget it, even if it had all been a dream. He missed the nymph, and he called out for her in his mind. Then he heard her voice in his head. She told him she had joined him in his heart so they could stay together — forever.

His wife was worried. She saw the storm and feared the worst. She was already mourning his loss when her husband came home. Her neighbor shouted that she saw a boat coming. To the woman's surprise, it was her husband. He was alive, and he looked better than he ever had before. She cried for hours and refused to let him go, afraid to lose him again. In the time afterward, their relationship improved. Both realized what being without the other did to them, how much they had missed each other. They grew closer and soon had their first child. A beautiful baby girl. A decade passed before the fisher's wife noticed something different. Her husband didn't age as much and weird things happened around her daughter. Fish gathered around the girl when she swam and the crops around their house were more massive than in the rest of the village. The woman couldn't explain it and her husband was blind to it, loving and adoring his little girl for all she did.

Years later the strange events stopped happening as the girl grew up and married a man from the city. The woman's health got worse, and the fisher took care of his wife. He only went fishing for a few hours each day, but he still brought back more than enough food every time. He told her stories of a faraway land where faeries lived and magic happened. She liked the stories and kept asking for more. He narrated them with incredible details, like he had been there before. She believed that he had. That this magical land was where he'd gone after the storm hit. She hoped she could visit the place after she was gone.

The man tried to sail back to the islands with his wife's ashes. Even though the warmth in his heart grew as he came closer, he never found them again. He scattered the ashes in the ocean, hoping that she would find them herself, as he once did.

Decapod's ire

The sun wasn't up yet, but Skylar was already dressed in his usual shirt and pants covered with studded leather pieces to protect him from sharp teeth. He grabbed his bow and quiver, hid the dagger in his boot, and went on his way. His parents were still asleep when he left. His father's presence was less pressing than Skylar's; Skylar was the one to protect the farmers. He had to be at his post before they arrived. He was one of the few archers who could successfully hit a wolf in the dark. The only thing he needed was a reflection in their eyes to know where to shoot. Throughout his years as a watchman he learned the habits of wolves.

As he walked down the hill, the scent of freshly baked bread met him.

"Good morning, Sky. Up early again?" The baker called.

"Always. I doubt they'll give me a different shift before my eyes go bad. So I could be doing this for another thirty years." Skylar smiled.

"Have some breakfast, on me. Without you I would be out of a job." The baker gave Skylar freshly baked bread straight out of the oven.

"Thank you, sir! I'll do my best to keep you your job as well as my own." He bowed and left the baker to his work.

Skylar gently put away the bread and headed towards the gate. It was still locked, and the bridge drawn up from the night before. He was the first to cross the rivers, like he should be. The guard shouted it was clear, but Skylar still drew an arrow, just to be sure.

The fields south of the city looked quiet. He couldn't hear anything but the whispers of the wind. Skylar walked over to the shed and grabbed some firewood to start a small fire. Once the fire burned brightly, he jumped on the shed, looking towards the forest where the wolves came from.

The wolves wouldn't come out now, but smaller animals would. They would eat the crops and predators would come for them.

These were the quiet hours. Skylar rarely saw the first farmers until the sun colored the sky. That's how he received his name. His mother loved this time of day, and so did he, after two years of the early watch. It didn't take long for the sky to change from a warm orange hue to a pale blue.

The farmers came in small groups to work the land. They waved at Skylar but didn't stick around for small talk.

The sun was out for a few hours when he heard the heavy boots of his father.

"Hey Sky, you can take a break now!" His father called. Skylar jumped down. He felt the bread in his pocket when he landed. He broke off a piece and gave it to his father.

"The baker gave me this on my way out, this morning." Skylar said before he ate his half.

"That's kind of him. I'll be sure to give him the best grain this season." Skylar's father was the overseer of these parts of the farmland and highly regarded by most of the citizens of Solhilde. He was a strong fighter, and his kindness knew no boundaries.

"Be good to other people, even when they can't give you anything in return. They, and others, will help you when you're in need." Skylar had seen his father do incredible things for people, asking for nothing in return. He admired this part of his father most of all.

The rest of the day was quiet. Skylar helped out on the field, the bow and quiver still on his back. Most of the farmers had weapons nearby, just in case. Predators rarely came out during the day, but being cautious had saved lives.

Dusk had fallen. Skylar was back at his spot on the shed. The light at this time of day was traitorous, colors faded and blended. Fires weren't bright enough to see clearly. Wolves often attacked at this hour.

The sound of birds flying away alarmed Skylar. Something was coming. He drew an arrow and kept his eyes on the forest. He cursed the sun for the lack of brightness. His father spotted his alertness and told the farmers to grab their weapons. A scream sounded farther up north, but it was too far away for Skylar to do anything. If it was a wolf, others would take care of it. The only thing he could do was keep the people around him safe. Most farmers were trained fighters, and their daily work kept them strong. Without the farmers, Solhilde would be without food.

Skylar noticed a shrubbery moving. He waited to see what caused it. A dark shadow ran out towards the fields. Skylar took aim and released the arrow. He heard a high whimper coming from the shadow. The large silhouette fell to the ground, but it kept trying to get back up. It wasn't dead yet. One of the farmers went over to see what it was.

"A wolf!"

The farmer took his dagger and slit the throat of the injured wolf.

"Tsk." Skylar drew another arrow. Two attacks from different paths, at least two packs on the hunt. He suspected there were at least seven more in the vicinity. A howl confirmed the presence of more wolves.

Two dead wolves was a big blow to the pack if it was small. Skylar hoped that it was enough to scare away the rest as it was getting darker. Farmers created fires at the edge of the farmlands since the clouds shrouded the moons. The fires were the only light they had.

Skylar peered into the forest, hoping to see shimmers of redness, a reflection of the fires. He only saw one set of eyes, blueish, higher from the ground. It could have been a tall man. It was unlikely for a man to be in the forest at this hour. He didn't notice any other wolves. One pack must've retreated after they killed a few.

Farther along, near his father's post, the farmers were still fighting. Skylar joined his father. There were six wolves in the field. Some were already hurt, but not enough to flee. He lined up an arrow to shoot the largest wolf. If he was lucky and killed the alpha, the others might retreat. The wolf, occupied by the man he was fighting, didn't know what was behind him. Skylar aimed for his flank, if the arrow passed through the ribs he could pierce its heart. He breathed out to steady his hand and let go of the arrow. That was all he could do.

The arrow struck the wolf. The wolf pulled the arrow out with its teeth and lunged at the man in front of him. Skylar's father was already on his way to finish the wolf, sword unsheathed. Skylar quickly shot another arrow to distract the wolf, but the arrow pierced its body near the old arrow. It pushed the arrowhead into its heart, killing it before his father even took a swing.

The beta let out a howl to warn the others. Most of them retreated, howling in return. There was one wolf that stayed behind. He was the smallest of the group, but also the fastest one, he only retreated after the others were already in the forest. The wolf dodged the attacks of the farmers with ease, as if he could predict them. Skylar felt a shiver go down his spine. Only after it was out of sight, he could relax.

His father cheered for their victory. Everyone joined in, except Skylar. He went back to his post as soon as the last wolf fell back. He peered into the forest to make sure they were retreating. Again he saw the blue eyes staring at him.

"You should relax and have a drink. They won't be back soon. You did well, son." His father climbed the storage with two pints of beer.

Skylar accepted a pint, but his expression remained the same.

"That beer won't attack you, you know. And you'll win in a stare down contest." His father tried to be funny, but his jokes never came out right.

Skylar shook his head. "I saw something in the forest. It wasn't a wolf, it was bigger."

"How do you know?" His father always took him seriously; he liked that about him.

"Its eyes were blue, and they were high up. Not in the tree branches but near there."

"That's... I don't believe we have a man that tall."

Skylar nodded. "The blue doesn't make sense either. They should reflect the light that shines in them, right? That's what you taught me. But there was no moon tonight, how could they reflect blue light? It doesn't make sense."

His father was quiet. Skylar could see he was thinking.

"I'll take a crew into the forest tomorrow morning. Maybe we can find some tracks or other evidence something was there." His father decided. "For now, I want you to finish that beer, sing a song, and go home. We need you back in the morning."

A smile appeared on Skylar's face—the first of the evening—and he drank his beer.

"Oh, one last thing. Where exactly did you see it?"

Skylar used his pint to point in the direction. "Straight ahead. As if it was watching me."

His father rested his hand on his son's shoulder. "Don't worry. Anything stupid enough to try to take you on dies when it gets in your sight. Your aim is sharp as you've proven again today."

* * *

The next morning was quiet. There were no more attacks, and Skylar relaxed during his watch. His father arrived late in the morning with a small group of hunters. He asked Skylar to shoot an arrow in the direction of the eyes when he was at the edge of the forest. Skylar had no idea how far into the forest the blue eyes were, but the arrow indicated where to look. A tree would've blocked his line of sight when he saw the eyes. He trusted his father to make sensible calls and to come back before dusk.

Later that afternoon Skylar noticed unrest with the farmers. The women often brought lunch and gossip, but this time he saw worry on many faces. He wasn't allowed to leave his post, and it bugged him not to know what was going on.

The women left, but the worried faces stayed. Skylar distracted himself by scouting the forest edge. He let out a sigh of relief when he saw his father coming back with his men, unharmed. At least something went well.

Skylar's father soon noticed the tension and asked the farmers what was going on. Several farmers were eager to share their worry with their leader. He listened to all of them and assured them he would find out what was going on. Skylar could read his father's body language like nothing else. He knew he would soon learn more.

His father came up to Skylar's post. "It's been a quiet day, eh?"

"Only on the forest side." Skylar couldn't deny the unrest on the fields.

"So you've noticed."

"Of course, why wouldn't I?"

"Your mother thinks you have the eyes of a hawk and an owl combined."

"It's no use to have the eyes of a hawk if you don't know what to do with what you see."

"You're right. Only a few more months until you're officially an adult, and you can do anything you want, but I secretly hope you'll stay with us. You can save many lives here with your eyes and your wit."

"I wasn't planning on going anywhere. I like it here. But tell me, my eyes might be sharp, but I don't have a bat's hearing. What are they talking about?"

"Some fishermen still haven't returned. Most of them only stay away for two or three days, but it's been a week now, and they're not home. Other fishermen haven't seen them either."

"How many boats?"

"Three. Three brothers who fish together to make the most profit. They take more risks than others, and I'm afraid it might have been fatal this time."

"You haven't told anyone you're suspicious?"

"No. I don't want to worry them even more. Yesterday's attack worried me as well. There were twelve wolves. With three dead, nine are left and they might form a bigger pack to hunt enough food for the coming winter. I'm worried I have to split up the men between the farm and the search if they don't turn up. We don't have enough men for both." The frown on his forehead grew bigger.

Skylar had never seen his father so worried. He admired him keeping his poise as a leader in front of the other men, but he opened up to Skylar.

"We'll see how it turns out. No use worrying over uncertain things." The man groaned when he stood up, stiff knees obstructing his mobility.

Skylar nodded. "Wait, what about blue eyes?"

"We found nothing, not even a print in the dirt. I believe you saw something, but all I can say for now is that it wasn't standing on the ground." His father shook his head. "Prepare for dusk. I hope it'll still be quiet."

* * *

The field and harbor were quiet the following days. There was still no trace of the fishermen. A few others had volunteered to head to their regular spot to see if they could find anything. The family of the fishermen gladly accepted. They only wanted to know what happened.

The scouting party returned a few days later. Skylar heard the townsmen talking when the women brought lunch. They only found debris of the boats, nothing else. It couldn't have been a storm; other fishermen would've noticed that. No storm is that local.

Skylar thought about those blue eyes. What if it was a monster? He didn't dare to say it, but he was sure his father would have considered it a possibility.

The quiet days and the unrest at sea inspired a few of the villagers to propose a wider search area. Five crews volunteered to search for the cause of the disappearance, while the other fishers were ordered to stay within eyesight of each other. It was the city council's decision, but everyone agreed.

A week later, the regular fishing boats returned while the search party was still out, minus one. A large tentacle—probably the same one that attacked the other boats—smashed it. They rescued the fishermen before they drowned.

The council called an emergency meeting. This was the first time a big threat happened on sea. They consulted the crew of the lost boat to help prepare for an assault.

Morale on the fields was low. Skylar noticed that the farmers didn't work as hard as they normally do. They grouped together discussing what they would do if it took one of them and if they should help with the search. Most of them left before dusk, afraid of a predator coming for them. It made Skylar think of what he could do to contribute.

The captain of one boat had already ordered reinforced plates for his boat, his crew was determined to catch the creature. He wanted to protect the hull so the creature couldn't break it from underneath. And if it wanted to attack from above water, the crew could take it out with weaponry. They had already ordered pikes, swords and a few tridents. Fishermen trained with farmers to learn the basics of combat, although their experience was with wolves and not gigantic sea monsters. What the fishermen needed was upper body strength, something the farmers could help with. Working on the fields was the easiest and most efficient way to gain strength while it simultaneously helped out the community.

Fish had become scarce the last month, and people needed more nutrition. Small groups ventured into the north side of the forest during the day to catch prey. More farmers joined the hunters, while fishermen who didn't take part in the search tried to fill in for the farmers. Farming didn't provide food right when it was necessary, and they needed food now. The hunters promised to help during the harvest season in return.

Skylar came home to his parents whispering at the dining table. They both had a rough week, but he had never seen them with such intense looks on their faces.

"What's wrong?" he asked.

"Ten crews are shipping out next week to kill the monster." His mother answered.

"And farmers are joining them, so we're losing men." His father added.

"I want to go too," Skylar said immediately.

"No, I need you on the field." The man looked intimidating with his arms crossed and a frown on his face.

"Dad, everyone is training for close combat, but they will be at sea. You want to kill it before it even reaches your boat. If it smashes your boat, you're done. They need people who can attack from farther away."

"He does have a point, dear." His mother said.

"You're actually okay with this insane idea?"

"No, of course not. I want him safe, but that doesn't mean

he's wrong." She put her hand on his arm and he relaxed a little.

"I'm the best archer in town. If I go, the chances the rest will come back will increase. Mother, you know that saving many is more important than a possibility of losing one."

"I know, but that doesn't make this any easier. You're our son. Let us be parents for a moment and worry. Then, we can be chief councilor and first field officer and tell you to help our men."

Skylar saw the worry on his parents' face. He hugged them. "Thank you for worrying. I'll do my best not to disappoint you. I'll be careful and listen to my superiors."

"That's what you should always do on a battlefield," said his father.

"I just want you to come back." His mother kissed him on the cheek, something she rarely did anymore.

Skylar felt the love of his parents, and they all knew that Skylar would be a great addition to the crew, despite his lack of seafaring knowledge.

Skylar's father asked his friend, Captain Lazlo to make Skylar part of his crew and educate him well. He told the captain he should be strict and treat his son like he would any other new recruit.

Captain Lazlo had a small crew of fifteen men who had been with him for over ten years. He hadn't trained a recruit since. He hoped that he still had the patience to mentor someone.

"I'll take care of your boy, Gharret. Don't worry." Captain Lazlo said when Skylar boarded.

"I won't. I trust you both to make the right decisions." Gharret shook hands with Captain Lazlo. "Just don't go easy on him. Let him experience real life at sea."

"I expect the best of my entire crew, new and old." Captain Lazlo looked at the group of hunters who had just arrived at the pier. "That should be the rest of the volunteers. I hope they can help us."

"The hunters are great fighters. Even more so than us farmers. I recognize this group, though. This is an elite hunting squad. They will know what to do and how to fight a monster," Gharret said.

"And they know nothing about life at sea, let alone battles at sea." Captain Lazlo wasn't convinced yet.

Gharret couldn't deny that.

"You'll be glad to have them when the fight starts, I'm sure. You might know about the sea, but the decisions you have to make in battle are different from when the sea is impetuous." Gharret hoped it was enough to encourage his friend to trust them.

"We'll see, Gharret. They'll get their chance to prove themselves." Captain Lazlo sighed and saluted before he went on board.

Gharret waved as the boat left the harbor. It was hard to see his son go, but it was for a good cause. He volunteered to protect the village. Soon enough he would be an adult and go his own way. This was just a first step.

* * *

Skylar saw three women shooting their bows at sea after he was done scrubbing the deck. He only noticed the ropes tied to the arrows when they pulled them back from the water. Dyon motioned for Skylar to join them.

"Come on. Grab your bow."

Skylar was confused. "What are you shooting at?"

"We visualize our target, since we have no idea what, or how big, the creature is. But we need to be able to aim well enough. Have you ever tried it?"

"No, not really. The wolves were target enough."

"You started with moving targets?" The wonder was visible on her face.

"Of course not. Their corpses were. My father took me out in the morning to practice. By the time I was old enough to join the evening shift, I was good enough to hit them up close."

"Huh. That's pretty smart."

The other two girls kept shooting at invisible targets, pulling the arrows back from the water.

"How many targets did you hit?" He asked one of them.

"All of them." She answered as she closed her eye to focus and aim. She released her fingers, and the arrow flew threw the air into the water.

Skylar felt something brewing in his stomach. Dyon tapped his shoulder with her bow and held it out. He accepted her offer, grabbed her arrow, aimed the bow straight forward, found his focus, and pulled back. He released his finger and waited.

Skylar opened his other eye and looked at the spot where he visualized his target. "That's where I aimed. Where is the arrow?" His mouth dropped staring at the target. His arrow wasn't there. He looked at Dyon to see if she noticed. Her hand was covering her mouth, but he could hear her laughing. She pointed to the front of the boat.

His glance followed the rope instead of Dyon's finger. The others were laughing as well. He finally found his arrow, almost in front of the boat.

His cheeks felt hot. He shoved the bow in Dyon's hands and

shuffled towards the kitchen when Dyon grabbed his arm.

"Wait. I get it. I know what went wrong and we can teach you."

Skylar didn't want to look at her, but he stopped walking.

"You didn't consider the wind," she said.

It took a moment for him to understand what she meant.

"The wind pushed your arrow out of the trajectory."

Skylar felt like an idiot. "I never even considered it."

"Yeah. You probably don't have to deal with it much on the farms. Wolves only attack when the wind is coming towards them. That way their smell doesn't reach their prey—you. So you always had the wind in your back when you needed to," Dyon explained.

"So they won't attack if the wind comes from their back. That makes sense." Skylar thought about the wolves. He didn't understand much of them. He wasn't a hunter, just a defender.

"You might be an excellent scout and sniper, but you're not a hunter. We're hunters. We chase the prey instead of defending our territory."

"What do you hunt?" Skylar was curious how she picked up her skill.

"Birds of prey, mostly. They kill the chickens. Other times we hunt deer or rabbits. Your mother buys our meat." Dyon crossed her arms and looked proud. Rabbits were hard to shoot, especially in the forest, but she was the best.

"Really? I didn't know."

"Well, you're always busy. If you're not at home, you're on the fields. You have no idea what's going on in town."

"You're right." Skylar let out a sigh. He knew his skills were limited, but he always thought he knew what was going on.

"It probably wouldn't hurt to get more involved in the town

business. I'm sure your mother won't mind educating you."

Dyon's comments confused him. He wasn't sure if she was trying to be nice or tell him he was sorely lacking in other aspects besides his work on the field. She knew everything, and she wasn't much older. Her expression was soft but stern. There was no bad intent in her words. He needed to trust her.

"Will you teach me how to shoot?" Skylar offered her her bow back.

"Of course. Use this bow. I've got others. Your bow isn't fit for this kind of shooting."

"How do you know?"

"You know there are different kinds of bows right?"

"Right." Skylar didn't want to admit that he didn't know.

"This is a recurve bow. It requires more strength, but the arrow has a higher velocity and hits the target straight. Your long bow arches your arrow. It's used for long range attacks and a lack of wind makes it easier to hit your target. This bow is for quick kills, under any circumstance. The bow is a gift, if you kill the creature with it." Dyon winked at him.

Skylar pulled the string back again. The resistance of the bow was more noticeable now. It was harder to pull it back as far as his own bow.

"Why didn't I notice it before?"

"Because your eyes were on the target and your hands focused on the arrow. You didn't take the time to get to know the bow."

Skylar felt slightly embarrassed. Ever since he was a kid, he had an affinity for archery. This was the first time he failed in a grand manner in front of other people besides his father.

Dyon put her hand on his shoulder. "Don't feel bad. There's one thing you can be certain of when you fail. You can always improve if you train long and hard enough."

She left him alone after saying those words. It was up to him now.

Skylar trained for three days, getting better each day. Dyon was watching him from a distance, but she never said anything. Skylar knew that she had already told him everything he needed to know. If he couldn't visualize the target, it was up to him to learn how. If he couldn't shoot the target, it was because he didn't anticipate the wind. He had to learn how to adapt to the wind. The best way to learn was to do it often.

Captain Lazlo had cleared him of his deck washing duties during the day so he could train, but only if he took first watch at night. Skylar said he would take the first two if he could sleep in the crow's nest. The summer still lingered, and Skylar preferred to sleep in the open air than the hammocks below deck, crowded with people.

On the fourth day the five boats grouped together. Captain Lazlo proposed that the hunters should be divided over all the boats. Most of the hunters were on his, but the others needed more ranged power, in his opinion.

The captain of the armored boat declined. He was all set and ready. His crew consisted of family members of those who were lost. They were filled with anger, and all of them were happy to take a swing at the creature. Their loss had made them a tight group, and most others were grateful not to be on that boat. They believed that the captain would sacrifice himself to kill it.

Dyon talked to her fellow hunters. They formed four groups. Dyon and Selia were together, Tyan and Emalin were another group, Selia and Marrela were the third, and Arba was to stay with Skylar.

"I don't care if you agree or not. This is how it's going to be," Dyon told Skylar afterward. "Arba is a fine archer herself, but she's no scout. I want you to scout for this boat. Tyan, Marrela, and I will scout for the others. The captain trusts your sight. I do too. Bring Arba home for me."

He only nodded, thinking he had no right to say anything about it. Maybe it's the nerves that hit him. He was part of the captain's crew, not the hunters. His duties aboard were mostly to scrub the deck and scout the waters, not to fight the monster. Although he and the captain both knew that was what he would do.

His stomach clenched together as he watched Dyon walk back to the other women. It couldn't be seasickness, not this late into their voyage. Mik came over and passed his pint with beer.

"You look like you could use this. Didn't like what she said?"

"I don't think it matters," he said as he accepted the pint.

"You could still disagree. Let it out, man. Y'll feel better."

"No, it's fine. I knew what I signed up for when I joined. We're going to kill that creature and we'll return safely."

"Y're not alone, kid. I might not look it, but my aim's pretty good. Not all fish we bring back are small, y'know." Mik clasped his large biceps to show it off.

"Thanks. I just hope I won't fail the captain. And the crew." He avoided Mik's piercing eyes.

"Trust your gut, and y'll be fine." Mik clasped Skylar's shoulder. "I've seen ye shoot. Nothing wrong with those eyes of ye."

"That's the problem. Right now, my gut tells me to jump overboard and swim back to shore."

"Well, y'r gut ain't wrong. Going back would be the smart

thing to do." Mik laughed. "Don't worry. Not yet, at least. The sea has taught me that running away ain't always the best option. Ain't the easiest either, mind ye. But together we can overcome problems. Learn to rely on others. Trust me to do me best, as the captain trusts ye."

"Thanks," Skylar said as he gave the pint back.

Mik only smiled and left him alone.

The uncomfortable feeling in his gut was still there, but it was quiet now. He no longer wanted to throw up. An image of his father popped up in his head. He would have said the same thing as Mik. We're not here to run; we chose to do this. Skylar knew he needed to get over this feeling, but how could he? The beer and the talk hadn't helped. Maybe he wasn't a fighter, but a defender.

He climbed back up to the crow's nest. It was empty since the sea was quiet. Skylar looked at the other boats; they were also waiting, preparing for the upcoming battle. That evening the hunters would take rowing boats to go to their new stations. Skylar knew it might be the last time he would see Dyon. Her smiles had become the highlights of his days. He stared at the horizon hoping to find the courage he was looking for. The courage to fight against this unknown creature, and to talk to Dyon. He wanted to, but he had no idea what to say. His mind became fuzzy thinking about her. He admired her, and she was his mentor the past few days. The feeling in his gut became worse again. It had to be related to Dyon's absence, but Skylar didn't understand why. He didn't want her to leave this boat, but why? He looked down. Her blond hair stood out among the browns and greens of the crew's clothes. Dyon had untied her braid. She almost never did. The one time he saw her with her hair loose, she was deep in thought and didn't respond until Skylar had nudged her. He wondered what she was thinking about.

After dinner, the crew brought extra supplies from the galley the hunters had to take with them. The others might not have enough to support the hunters' needs. Two small boats carried the archers and supplies to the other boats.

Skylar had a hard time saying goodbye to his new friends; he hoped he would see them again. Arba stood next to him and hugged her friends goodbye. He saw the tears on her cheeks but felt it wasn't his place to comfort her. They had become closer, but he was still an outsider to their group.

His stomach became upset when Dyon climbed over the railing. He saw her smiling at him. It was a sad smile, not the ones he had seen before. It pained him. He clenched his fists to redirect his feelings.

They would enter the waters of the second attack any day now. Everyone needed to be alert, the scouts especially. Skylar had a job to do, and he couldn't afford to be distracted.

Later that night he gazed at the stars from his crow's nest. He knew what he had to do. Focus on the horizon and the waters. The sailors had taught him the basics of ocean weather to make it easier for him to understand patterns. He had learned how to recognize abnormal behavior in the water as a school of dolphins swam around them. He hoped he could use that knowledge to fight this creature and protect his people.

* * *

"There! The water is bubbling. It has to be there." One of the navigators shouted. The waves were rough compared to that morning. Even the wind was stronger, and the sun disappeared behind the clouds. As if the world knew what was about to happen.

The five re-purposed fishing boats spread out, and the crew prepared for assault. Skylar clenched the bow to his chest. He hoped the wind would honor his wishes and stay away, but he was thankful for Dyon's lessons. He was grateful to have her bow even when she transferred to another boat. It made sense to spread the elite hunters instead of keeping them together. Maybe now they had a chance to take it out.

A burly crew member carried a harpoon to the front of the boat while Skylar climbed to the crow's nest. It was up to him to spot an opening to attack from this distance. It was still twice the distance he could hit in these weather conditions.

Dyon waved at him from the boat to his left. He signaled good luck back. She was their spotter, and Skylar knew she would do a better job. He hoped they would both survive, and that he could join her hunting group to hone his skills.

The water in front of the boat started to ripple. Sleek dark skin became visible on the surface. All eyes were on the creature. It didn't move, and it was impossible to see what part of its body had surfaced. It looked like the top of a sphere. Maybe like a tortoise's shell, but round. A huge wave emerged from behind the boat closest to the creature. A large tentacle appeared and struck the boat. The men shot the harpoons as the tentacle came nearer. A few of them hit, but it wasn't enough to repel the attack. The tentacle, thicker than two grown men hugging, struck the mast and crushed the cabin. Three men fell overboard, and the boat closest threw ropes to help them get on board.

Two brave men swung their swords at the tentacle. It didn't bleed, but Skylar could see they injured the creature. The boat had barely survived the attack. Another hit could sink it.

The armored boat made headway to the dark smooth part of the creature. Spikes attached to the boat could hurt it badly if they could pick up speed. Skylar kept looking at the body, letting the others deal with the tentacles. The sphere moved, fresh water slid off the emerging surface. He noticed a white line around the sphere, where the smooth surface was covered by a layer of skin. It reminded Skylar of a tuna's skin instead of a tortoise shell. He looked at the sea surrounding the creature. There were light and dark spots, but the water between Skylar's boat and the visible part of the creature was all dark. Large blobs drifted towards the other boats.

The creature was underneath them. The thing sticking out of the water was its eye. The whole creature was longer than all boats combined.

Fear overtook him. He wasn't sure what to do or call. He doubted if they could kill it. They only barely damaged one of its tentacles, and there were at least seven more.

"Boy, what do you see?" Captain Lazlo asked.

Skylar knew he had to say something. They depended on him, and for once he wasn't the one who could save them.

"The creature, it's underneath us all. That thing is its eye, and we only saw one of the tentacles. Prepare for anything because I have no idea where it will attack next." Skylar tried to give an accurate overview of the situation without scaring the crew.

"What of the others?"

"One boat is damaged, but they repelled attack and injured the tentacle. The other boat is charging the eye."

"Do they know that the thing is its eye?"

"I doubt it. The captain is filled with rage and probably made a rash decision. If it works and they take out the eye, it will go wild and the tentacles underneath us will try to swipe at us."

"Should we move?"

"I think it would be best to move northwest. That way we'll be closer to its core, and the tentacles probably won't reach there."

"Then that's what we'll do. Remind me to thank your father for giving you a good brain." Captain Lazlo saluted him and went towards the wheel.

Skylar was grateful for the captain's trust, but he also felt the weight of it. If his judgment was wrong, he had to deal with the consequences. He had seen it before on the farms where a spotter had made a wrong call, and his friend died. The spotter never fully recovered from it. Skylar's father had explained that such responsibilities aren't for everyone. If you could put past mistakes aside and focus on the present, only then could you be a good leader.

Skylar trained under his father for years before he was allowed to man a station alone. He was confident in his skill, but the sea wasn't the edge of the forest, and wolves were ants compared to this monster. All of this was new.

He glanced in Dyon's direction to see what she was doing. She had her bow ready and kept checking every direction. Probably trying to spot if one of the tentacles came up again. Their eyes met, and Skylar pointed toward the sea between them and gestured they were tentacles. Then he pointed towards the eye of the monster and then his own, hoping she would understand. She raised her arms above her head and shaped an 'O'. She had, and she didn't seem scared at all.

He wished they could talk strategies right now. Signing only got you so far. What would they do, as hunters? He knew that there were other, bigger predators in the woods than wolves, but they rarely showed their faces. Hunters had to be ready for anything and not assume that they were at the top of the food chain.

The boats to the left approached the eye, one boat was still picking up speed as it drove the spikes into the eye. The soft membrane ripped and murky liquid came gushing out. The tentacles breached the water behind Skylar. He looked at the captain who gave him a thumbs up; he had made the right call. Five tentacles were thrashing around, none of which injured, Skylar noted. Waves crashed against the back of the boat, pushing them towards the head. It was almost in range now. The head of the creature was turning. Slowly the injured eye disappeared, and its other eye became visible.

"There's the other eye. We have to blind it." He called to Mik.

One arrow wouldn't be enough to penetrate it. He doubted arrows would even be effective against the colossal monster. He pulled an arrow out of the quiver and inspected the tip. The metal had a sheen he didn't recognize. He brought the tip closer to his nose, the smell of poison greeted. He thanked his gut feeling not to touch the tip. Dyon should've warned him. He looked back to see how she was doing.

Tentacles whipped at the boat, obscuring his view. It didn't look good. They were surrounded, and Skylar couldn't help them. He could only hope.

"Oy! Skylar, should we go closer?" the captain called. He almost forgot they were in danger, even if it wasn't immediate.

"No, let's wait here to see if the harpoon can reach the eye. We don't know how big the head is. I'm guessing one head butt is enough to break the boat." Skylar signaled it was okay to shoot if Mik agreed.

"No, we need to get closer. I'm afraid I won't hit hard enough from this distance."

The captain was already steering in the right direction. Water bubbled in front of the boat.

"Watch out, something is happening." Skylar pointed, and the captain turned the wheel to the other direction.

The creature's darkness loomed closer to the surface. Skylar saw a light spot between all the dark. It was just next to the boat as it broke the surface. The beak opened and tried to attack the boat.

Skylar quickly shot an arrow into the open beak. He wasn't sure if it hit, but at least one poisonous arrow was inside. One graze was enough to get the poison into its system.

Mik was still aiming at the eye, but the rocking off the boat made it difficult.

"Mik, shoot the damned thing. It's trying to eat us." The captain ordered.

"I'm trying, but it's too far away."

"Shoot in its beak. We won't blind him, but he won't like it either. The others are closer and they still have harpoons left. We should focus on doing as much damage as we can." Skylar said. Mik nodded and ran to the other side of the boat. One of the other guys grabbed a keg of gunpowder.

"Should we blow him up?"

"Can't hurt to try," the captain said.

"Oh, I'm hoping it'll hurt."

"Just make sure the fuse is long enough. I don't want to blow up my own boat." Captain Lazlo grumbled.

Skylar shot more arrows into the beak and hoped that the harpoon or the bomb would allow the tip of the arrow to enter the body.

The harpoon had successfully penetrated the upper half of the beak, while the barrel exploded just outside causing only a part of the beak to break off. It hurt the creature enough to charge back. One of its other tentacles rose from the sea and curled around the boat. The men picked up their swords and Skylar kept shooting arrows.

Screams alerted him to look back. The creature had finally shown itself completely. It was a giant squid with three large eyes.

One on each side of its head. They were large enough to cover the sides of its head with only a small piece of skin between them. The beak looked even more monstrous now, damaged and covered in its dark blood.

"We're leaving. Skylar, which way out is the safest?" the captain yelled.

"What? We can't leave, it's not dead." Skylar turned to the captain.

"Boy, do you see that thing? It's gigantic. We can't kill it. Not even with an army of sharks. We have to go. I won't throw away our lives."

"We owe it to the others." He wanted to stay and fight. He never ran from an attack.

"You still have to learn how to pick your battles. If we lose everyone, it'll be a total defeat and no one will know what happened. If we go back, we might have a chance next time. Don't be stupid. Which way?" the captain was already steering away from the creature. The waves the tentacles caused pushed the boat into the right direction.

"We have to go around. Its eye on the left is damaged and it might miss us trying to get away." Skylar knew he had orders to obey, but he couldn't ignore the feeling in his stomach either. He climbed down the crow's nest, grabbed the spare harpoon, yanked the crossbow out of the Mik's hand and went back up. The captain called him out, but he ignored it.

Skylar aimed for one of the eyes. If he hit the eye, it would be another battle won, and the others had a better chance to escape. One lost harpoon was worth the risk. Success would mean more lives saved.

The waves kept rocking the boat, and the wind was stronger on this side. He thought back to Dyon's lessons. He listened to the rhythm of the waves as he felt the wind on his cheek. His only luck was that the creature was huge. The targets he used during practice were much smaller, and he managed to hit those.

The captain spotted Skylar taking aim at the eye and ordered his men to go closer if possible. Skylar slowed his breathing and shot. The harpoon flew through the air, and the boy held his breath. It hit the corner of the left eye; the tip was in.

Two of the eyes were blind, the beak was damaged, and poisoned arrows were in its system. A few of the tentacles were injured, maybe even more now since he hadn't seen what happened at the other side. Skylar didn't think they were losing, but it wasn't over yet. The captain was right to take this win and go for the kill another time. He couldn't see the other boats since the creature was in between them. The waves and splashes were an indication it was still thrashing around with its tentacles. Skylar hoped Dyon was still alive. Once they passed by its head, he saw three boats fighting tentacles. The boats were damaged, and he thought he saw people in the water.

"We have to help them." He shouted to the captain.

"We did. We blinded another eye. Going in won't assure

that we'll save them." Captain Lazlo stood near the railing and looked at the ongoing battle. Skylar knew the captain wanted to help them and that this was his responsibility. Knowing when to make the hard decision.

Skylar grumbled and tried to look for Dyon's boat. There was a deafening sound from his left side. It was the creature, which had been badly hurt. That's when Skylar saw a boat close to the beak, smoke was coming from the creature. The creature turned and dipped its beak under water, its only working eye turned towards the boat. Skylar saw something flying towards the eye, but the creature was too slow to turn away from the projectile. It exploded on impact. The third eye was now injured, and it had no vision.

That was enough to force it underwater. The tentacles slowly pulled back, and the head disappeared back into the ocean in a sad retreat. Skylar felt sorry for it, until he thought about the men who hadn't come back from their fishing outing.

It took a few minutes before the ocean calmed down. The captain steered towards the closest boat, where two men had fallen overboard and held on to the wreckage of the masts. Skylar went down to help pull them on board.

All five boats had survived, but they had taken a battering. Two lost their sails and wouldn't make it home. It was best to divide all the people on the two boats that could make it home.

Dyon's boat was good enough to survive the journey home, just like his. Skylar wanted to be with her. He was eager to find out what happened on her side, but he had to be patient. Patience was usually one of his strong suits, but not when it came to her. There was an attraction he didn't recognize. Just five nights until they were home.

* * *

Back at the harbor the captains conferred and made a report of what happened before heading to the council. Other townsmen welcomed them back, most of them crying of joy to see their loved ones again. Skylar's mother was there, and she hugged him tightly.

"I was so afraid. When they said there were only two boats returning, I feared the worst. But I never expected so many of you to come back." She had tears in her eyes, like all the other family members.

Skylar scouted the area for Dyon, but she was already gone.

"Mom, I'm glad to be back, but I have to go. We'll talk later okay?" Skylar had missed his father and needed his advice.

She nodded. "I'm sure the council will be called soon. Go visit your father at the farms. He was even more afraid than I was, although he never expressed it."

Skylar grabbed his two bows and quiver and headed towards the fields. Maybe his father knew what to do.

His father pulled him into a big hug, and other farmers patted him on the back and congratulated him. Some had already heard the creature had died. Skylar still wasn't sure if that was true, but he didn't want to spoil the mood. Once things had calmed down a bit, Skylar told his father everything and showed him his new bow.

"Wow, this is beautiful. The finish is well done, and the carving shows excellent craftsmanship. Who gave it to you?" His father inspected the bow carefully.

"Dyon, one the hunters. She showed me how to use it, how to take the wind into consideration, and the differences in bows. She taught me so much I didn't know, and it made me realize that I'm only good at sniffing out wolves." Skylar looked down and fidgeted with his shirt.

"Sky, you're only sixteen winters. No one expects you to have mastered one thing, let alone more. It's already an accomplishment you're this good. Don't be too hard on yourself." He gave the bow back and sat down.

"She isn't much older than me but she's much better. She can do everything I can, but better." Skylar tightened his grip on the bow.

"Well, if you feel that way, there's only one thing you can do." His father grinned.

Skylar looked up. "What's that?"

"Learn more. Ask the hunters if you can join them for a year and learn everything you can."

"You don't mind?" His eyes grew wide.

"Of course not. We'll miss you, but we managed when you were at sea. You're young, you should learn as much as you can. Promise me you'll come back though. I missed seeing your face around here. Your mother missed you as well, but she won't tell you." His father looked proud.

"I'm back, and if it's up to me, I won't go back on a boat any time soon. Even when I'm with the hunters, I'll be home for dinner so you won't have to miss me so much." Skylar was excited. He didn't expect his father to suggest him training with the hunters, nor would he suggest it himself.

"Your mother will be happy. Dinners without you were quiet."

"I should probably find Dyon, right? Maybe she doesn't want me there."

"Why wouldn't she? She already taught you so much, and she gave you her bow. She knows how good you are."

"I don't know. That was different; we had a monster to kill.

Without her lessons, I would've been worthless. She's amazing. Why should she spend her time with a simpleton like me?"

"Who's the simpleton? Why are you saying that?"

"Compared to her I'm nothing. She's the one who killed the creature while I did nothing. If she hadn't poisoned the tips, I wouldn't have hurt it at all. If she didn't teach me how to use this bow or how to read the wind, I wouldn't have done any damage at all." Skylar rattled on. He felt warm inside, and the pressure in his head was building up.

"I'm sure there are things she can learn from you too. Do you remember that just a few moments ago dozens of people came up to you to welcome you back?" His father gestured to the men working behind them.

"Yeah, but they don't know I didn't kill it."

"They welcomed you back with such enthusiasm because of what you did in the past. You were already one of the best men out there. And not because you won a battle. You've won many, and you're a decent guy. You're not only judged by what you know or do, but also how you treat others. Your mother and I fought to be in a leadership position; we couldn't have done it without the support of others. Your success is what you make of it, don't look at one moment in time. Others don't either. Dyon can be a great hunter, the best, but if her personality is rotten, she's not someone to follow."

"You're right," Skylar sighed. "By the way, did you ever find out more about what I saw?"

His father crossed his arms and closed his eyes. "We went into the forest that day and didn't find anything. I went back later and found a large paw print, but it was nowhere near where you indicated."

"Could it have been a wolf?"

"This paw print was twice the size of a regular wolf's paw. It must have been a gigantic wolf if it was one."

Skylar nodded, glancing at the forest.

"Good. Now let's head back to town to hear the council. I'll come back here to tell the others afterward. And you should find the hunters." His father patted Skylar's back.

When they reached the town plaza, nearly the entire village was there, except for the ones who couldn't leave their employ. The council and the captains were standing at the center near the well, with Skylar's mother in the middle of the group.

"Friends, I'm sure everyone already knows that our seafaring brothers and sisters have returned victorious." She started her speech. The whole square cheered when she said the last word.

"We have heard the stories of the captains, and we're blessed that many of them made it back. We lost five dear friends: Marric, Davon, Selia, Tyan, and Melvin. The decapod, as the creature is dubbed by the captains, killed them trying to destroy the boats. They counted ten tentacles, three eyes, one large beak, and it's larger than our village from the bridge to the harbor. I commend our brave fighters to fight such a monster and return with so few losses."

Skylar covered his ears as everyone was cheering and he felt hands patting his back to congratulate him. His father looked at him proudly.

"There is one individual I would like to name for her exceptional contribution in battle. Dyon, would you join us for a minute?"

His father gave him a look with raised eyebrows. People around him whispered curious to who the girl was.

The tall girl walked towards the center. Skylar recognized

her green eyes, but a leather mask covered the rest of her face and her hair was hidden beneath a leather cap. Dyon already wore her hunter's armor. Large leather chest pieces and pads on her thighs to protect her from tusks and teeth. Skylar's mouth dropped.

Dyon removed her face mask so people could see her. Her bow resting on her back.

"I'm glad you came here before your hunt. I heard you were the one who killed the decapod."

Dyon was quiet for a minute. "It's true I landed the finishing blow, but it was a group effort. Everyone did their part. From distracting the tentacles, to blinding the eyes. If anyone should get extra recognition, it's Skylar."

People gasped and turned around to look at him. These whispers differed from the ones when Dyon was called forward. People knew he was as the son of the chief of council and the first field officer.

Skylar felt his father give him a push in the council's direction. "Go," he whispered.

"Skylar was the one who blinded two of the three eyes. He gave me the idea to use gunpowder to blast the beast apart from the inside. If he didn't give me those ideas, I wouldn't have killed it. He distracted the decapod enough to save our boat and his own. But without the help of the whole crew, we wouldn't have done anything. We should celebrate everyone today, especially those we couldn't save."

Dyon took a bow and walked away.

"Dyon is right. Tonight we will celebrate the lives of all that have lost theirs to the decapod, now and before."

The crowd cheered again. Skylar took it as his cue to leave and headed towards his father. His father looked at him with big eyes and waved that he should follow Dyon. Skylar nodded and left towards the eastern city gate.

Dyon wasn't in a hurry, and Skylar caught up with her after a few blocks.

"Hey Dyon, wait. I want to ask you something." Skylar stopped running a few paces behind her. Dyon turned around, her face covered by the mask again. Skylar didn't like not being able to see her expressions in a conversation, but he didn't want to waste this opportunity either.

"I want to come with you." He walked towards her but kept three paces between them.

"That doesn't sound like a question." Dyon crossed her arms. It made her look intimidating in full armor.

"You've shown me how much I still have to learn, and I know you can teach me. Please let me join you for a year to learn everything I can." He pleaded but hoped his sincerity showed.

"What makes you think you can join my unit?" Her eyes didn't tell him much about what she thought or how she felt.

"I shot the targets just as well as your friends."

"So you want to join an all female hunting unit just because you can shoot an arrow?"

Skylar blushed. He never considered their group was women only. They never mentioned it.

"Haha, I fooled you." Dyon's laugh sounded muffled behind the mask, but Skylar saw the laughing wrinkles in the corner of her eyes.

"It's true my unit is all female, but that's only because no other hunters have our skill. Come with me, and I'll introduce you to someone else. He can teach you. After the winter is over, you can come with us for a hunt to test your skills. If I deem you worthy, I will personally train you." She said and gestured for him to follow her.

"Why after winter?"

"One of our girls is with child, and I want her to stay close to town in her last trimester. It's safer. She's our scout, so you can earn her spot."

They crossed the bridge, and Skylar saw the hunter's camp for the first time. It was larger than expected. Fires were burning to roast meat, and dead animals hung from the trees. He even saw a few familiar faces. These were the men who came to get the wolf corpses. Only now did he notice the amount of wolf skins hanging around.

In the middle of the camp was a bigger bonfire and an open tent. A large table was set up in the middle, with paper covering the entire surface. Dyon walked in and introduced Skylar to the biggest man he had ever seen. He was twice as broad as his father and twice his mother's height.

"Skylar, meet your new master, Marcus. Marcus, this is the boy I told you about before the meeting. Make him sweat, we need him later." Dyon pushed him towards Marcus. Her strength surprised Skylar.

The man appeared to be the same age as his father, although gray hairs lined his full beard already. Marcus held out his hand. Skylar shook it, his hand almost crushed.

"Ah, delicate archer's fingers. I'm sorry. You're Gharret's boy, aye? Welcome." His laugh bolstered throughout the tent. Marcus guided Skylar out of the tent as he explained the house rules.

Skylar looked over his shoulder to see Dyon waiting in the tent. It would be two seasons until he would see her again, if he completed the training.

Lovers across time

There was a man who could jump in and out of time. He could travel back in time to witness historical events and even go to the future. There was one restriction: he couldn't travel to the same moment twice. It was only the moment of arrival he couldn't jump to. He tried again and again, but the closest he could travel was five minutes apart.

Traveling through time made him experience time vastly different from his peers. His life was counted in hours instead of days. The time of arrival after a jump wasn't always the same as when he left. He could jump at night and arrive in the morning sun. He saw more sunrises than most people of the same age since he could jump to that time whenever he wanted. He learned to live listening to his body's need instead of watching the sun's position. He slept when he was tired, and he ate when he was hungry.

He met the love of his life traveling back in time, on a village square he accidentally walked into. It was his first time jumping back an excessive amount of time, and he hadn't planned on meeting people. But there she was, selling her father's fruits. That year's crop was one of their best. The strawberries were glowing, and the melons were the size of a child's head. She urged him to buy some and let him taste a strawberry for free. She smiled at him when he said they were heavenly. He fell in love immediately. With her smile. Her auburn hair reflected gold in the sun. Her eyes were deep dark wells in which he could see himself. The sound of her voice was enchanting. Whenever he ate strawberries, he thought of her.

He jumped back in time often so they could meet and learn about her village. It was important to know what he could and couldn't say and what they knew about what happened outside the village.

He tried living in her time, but he couldn't. He was used to certain technologies that weren't invented yet, and it was hard to not talk about things he considered a normal part of life. So he traveled back and forth a lot, just to see her. In the meantime, he researched his abilities, logging every trip he made with the approximate date, although he did not always know the precise date.

After a year had passed in his lover's time, she started talking about marriage and children. She wanted to get married as soon as possible and have five children. He knew he needed an heir to pass on his gift, but he didn't want to betray both of their feelings. She wanted a proper marriage. She wanted him settled down with her, but he needed to know more before he could decide what was best. Not just for him, but for all of his descendants. He took it upon himself to write a book with all his knowledge about his time traveling power, the possibilities and general history. He worked on a family tree, general limitations of the gift, and all the aspects of the time wandering lifestyle. It was by no means a must to use the power. There have been many before who lived their lives without ever using it. The man thought some of his ancestors didn't even know they had this power. His research would be wasted if some distant cousin inherited the gift but not the knowledge he had accumulated. He wanted his child to inherit this legacy.

That's when he told her, slowly, who he was and where he came from. He explained small parts during their meetings and not everything at once. This way, she wouldn't be scared off immediately, she had time to process it and to think of questions. His method worked, and she said it didn't change how she felt about him.

They still met, but it was different. She became more distant although she asked him to stay with her and live his life like his father and his father's aunt every time they spoke. He knew he would never love another woman as much as he loved her. That's when he experimented with transporting living things between times. If only he could transport her, they could always be together, no matter what time they went to. They would be time nomads until they found a time and place to call home.

After some experimenting, he told her what he'd been trying to do. She said she would help him if he needed her. A year later they were ready to try the first time jump together. They would jump five minutes ahead in time. Not much could go wrong there. None of the animals were hurt during the experiments. Some didn't come along, but they still existed in their original time. They made the jump and both came through. A day later they were married.

Throughout the years they looked for a place and time to settle and start a family, but it was hard. Either it was too far apart from her age or his. She eventually became pregnant, and they had to settle. They decided they would go closer to his age, but settled in a village where modern inventions were a luxury. They wouldn't be close to the center of the village, but close enough to get to the market and back within a day. The newlyweds didn't want to attract much attention in the village, afraid for slipping up when asked a question.

The woman gave birth to three children, the twin girls came first and later a boy. The man didn't know who would inherit his gift, so he wanted to educate them all on what he knew. He started telling them stories when they were five years old, to make them understand the concept of time. Only when they understood, he took them for a trip to the past. Meanwhile, his wife made sure she raised the children to be good, respectable people and taught them everything about farming, trading, and haggling.

They both educated their children about different subjects. When the twins saw their tenth spring, the man decided it was time for all three to read his research. He saw his eldest daughter had the most potential and understanding of the gift. The youngest told her parents she wasn't interested in the gift. She wanted to be a teacher, inspired by her mother's teachings.

Three years passed. The man believed the children knew all there was to know. Even his youngest wanted to know how it worked, even though she didn't want to be trained in using the gift. He still made his occasional trip to the past, taking his wife to visit her parents, or visit the future, to visit his mother.

On one of his trips to the future, the man picked up from a messenger that the capital had sunken into the ocean. This never happened in his timeline. History had changed, for the worst. He wasn't sure why it happened, what caused it, or if it was their fault. He told his wife he needed to investigate what happened. He left his research behind for his children in case he never returned. The man stepped out of the cottage, jumped a week back in time, and traveled towards the citadel, Solhilde.

The man headed towards the next village to buy provision. In his haste, he had only brought a bag with some clothes, a mantle, and fire sticks. He needed more food. The man was in luck.

There was a merchant traveling to the capital who invited the time traveler to join him. The journey would be safer with two and much faster than if he traveled alone. The merchant had a donkey and a cart for his wares, but not much more. He lent his travel companion a dagger to defend himself and his company, just in case.

He could use his powers to get to the capital faster, but he made the conscious decision not to. He still didn't know what happened if he used his power excessively and he wanted to use the time to figure out what happened. The merchant heard much during his travels, and often people asked him for the latest news. Every night he shared stories of what was going on. At least the man knew what he could expect before he arrived at the capital.

Five days later the two men arrived at the capital. The man wanted to return the dagger, but the merchant refused to take it back. No, it would serve him well here, since crime had increased over the last months. As an outsider he would certainly be a target for thieves and pickpockets. He needed it more than the merchant. The man thanked him and prepared for the worst.

He headed out early the next day. He walked around crowded places, hoping to pick up some gossip about what was going on. The market wasn't the place for such gossip, nor was the government building. He did see some people acting suspiciously, like they were sharing secrets and gossip. Two women in expensive clothes were whispering behind their fans. They headed towards a seamstress shop. He followed them inside.

The assistant came to him and wondered why a man would enter their shop. He explained that he had two young girls. They were to be women soon, and he wanted to spoil them with the most beautiful dresses. The two women who entered overheard him and asked him to tell more about his daughters, curious to know who would enter society soon. The assistant also wanted to know more about them, such as their sizes and what color their hair was. The man was embarrassed because he didn't know their sizes and apologized. He answered that his daughters looked very much like one of the ladies, who had a petite frame, except for her beauty. His daughters still had too much of a child physique to be considered a beauty by men. The woman blushed. The man asked if she minded being measured for the dresses. She was all too pleased to be of any assistance.

He talked with the women all afternoon and asked if he could take them out for tea, except he didn't know where. One of the women proposed they could have tea at her house, just around the corner. The size of the house surprised the man. The women giggled as the man almost tripped while being distracted by a large portrait in the hallway. They knew he was from out of town since he didn't recognize them. The petite woman confessed to be the mayor's wife.

The man eased his way into political gossip by saying he hoped his girls would marry well and that his son would be an apprentice. The women immediately told him they would take his daughters under their wings, and they would find suitable candidates for them. The women knew everyone, and their secrets. A list of potential suitors was already in the works.

As for the apprenticeship, they weren't sure. They discussed which politician would be the best. Slowly the power struggle in the government became clear. One of the chancellors used magic to attain power within the council. Others feared him and the repercussions his abuse of power and magic would have. The women thought this chancellor was behind the increased crime and shortage on fish.

The hostess asked the man if he wanted to stay for dinner and get to know her husband. The man declined and said he had different business to attend to. He needed to get out of the city, beyond the gates, before the capital sank. He knew it would happen when the sun went down.

A few hours later, the man was sitting at the top of the hill on the other side of the river. He heard a low sound and felt tremors not much later. Then, it happened. Everything on the piece of land between the rivers disappeared. It looked like the ground crumbled away, and the water swallowed it. It didn't look magical, but something was definitely wrong. He wasn't allowed to tell anyone it was going to happen, and he was sad he couldn't save his new friends.

Acknowledgements

It's been a long journey since I first penned down my ideas for this collection. I had plans and those plans changed at least a dozen times. Years passed even after I decided these nine stories were part of the first volume. But I'm incredibly proud and grateful this collection is out into the world and that you're reading this.

I couldn't have done this without the help and support of many people. I'm grateful to my parents for encouraging me to read, read and read some more. They normalized reading and let me borrow anything from the library.

Special thanks go out to my friend Raven van Dijk, who believed in me and my writing. He has also helped me with editing and provided feedback to help create this world. Without him, I probably wouldn't have pushed myself to write more, better, and aim for publishing.

I want to thank Anna Reel for editing the stories in between her busy schedule and her lovely comments. Her upbeat attitude helped me get over some of the anxiety of showing my creation to world.

My sister created the cover, which is absolutely gorgeous. Her whimsical style fit with the animals that I had in mind. It's almost scary how in sync we are sometimes.

Most of all, I want to thank my husband, Flo, for helping me with the publishing part of the process. Publishing this book would've taken another three years without him. His—and Shiro's—support motivated me to keep going and aim for my goal, publishing my first book. No doubt that many more will follow.

Thank you for reading

If you like Tales of Lunis Aquaria, consider rating and/or leaving a review on a retailers' website or GoodReads.

Sign up to Tessa's newsletter to stay up to date with future publications in the world of Lunis Aquaria. You'll receive up to four mails a year.

Follow Tessa on Twitter (@endalia) or read her blog (www.narratess.com) where she posts every Friday.

About the Author

Tessa Hastjarjanto is a Dutch/Indonesian writer from the Netherlands. She writes speculative fiction, and blogs at narratess.com about books, fountain pens, and writing.

From a young age, she imitated popular stories and games in creating her own worlds. This love eventually led to a master's degree in media and game studies at the University of Utrecht. However a mundane desk job was enough to inspire her to follower her creative passion. The first fanfics were written in lunch breaks and soon original fiction followed.

With the support of her husband, she now focuses on her writing career while battling chronic pain. Swiss white shepherd, Shiro, acts as a therapy dog to keep her healthy and reduce stress through extensive cuddle sessions.

Check out her author page at tessahastjarjanto.com.

You can connect with me on:
- http://www.tessahastjarjanto.com
- http://www.twitter.com/endalia
- http://www.facebook.com/tessahastjarjanto
- http://www.narratess.com

Made in the USA
Middletown, DE
04 September 2022

72656436R00071